The Maze from Hell: A Backrooms Tale

By CG Heandez

Trigger warnings: mild sexual content and age gap romance. There are little to no sexual triggers in this book but recommended for 18 & over)

Content

Summary

On a summer's day, Aleena, a 21-year-old woman, made plans to attend Comic-Con with two of her friends. Unbeknownst to her, an unforeseen and perilous adventure awaited, plunging her into a surreal realm where logic is turned upside down and escaping seemed nearly impossible. While trapped in the maze from Hell, she will encounter an unexpected ally, and together they must navigate through the infamous Backrooms to stay alive.

In the depths of the Backrooms, a treacherous domain unfolds,
Its insatiable grip pulls you deeper into its labyrinthine heart,
A non-Euclidean expanse where the very walls seem to shift,
Shadows dance and flicker, concealing the horrors that lie in wait.
Whispers echo through the corridors, a chilling symphony of dread,
As unseen entities stalk your every step, their intentions shrouded in malice.
Trapped in this merciless realm, where hope is but a fleeting memory,
And despair weaves itself into the fabric of your very soul.

1

The Peasant Girl

Aleena strolled along the shoreline, basking in the warmth of the summer afternoon. The invigorating salty breeze danced through her long, naturally wavy dark brown Auburn hair, adding to the bliss of the moment. She sported a set of denim shorts matched with a relaxed white cotton blouse featuring charming floral embroidery, finished off with brown sandals. As she took the white polkadot scrunchie off her wrist, she swept her hair back into a casual ponytail. Her friends were busy with their own commitments and couldn't join her at the beach, but she yearned for a peaceful escape anyways. She sought to find her inner calm while reflecting on the exciting adventures that await her this Summer. *"The Comic-Con is set to take place in San Diego this summer, which is exciting, can't wait to go. The rest of the summer days will be carefree and peaceful.,"* she mused. While the summer would certainly be peaceful and a great time to hang out with her friends, she remains unaware that her life is about to change forever. She exhaled deeply, taking in the sight of people relishing their summer afternoon. After an hour of enjoying herself at the beach, she made her way back to her car and drove home. Later, her friends Liz and Tiki arrived, and they spent time

together, chatting and watching TV. “Are we going to Comic-Con this year?” Tiki asked. Yep, let’s make plans for a two-day adventure there,” Aleena suggested. Aleena and her friends chatted about their summer plans, and once they departed, the family relaxed for the evening. At 21, she was still living at home, a situation that was becoming increasingly common as rising living costs made it tough for typical college students to afford their own place. She is indifferent to the situation; living at home allowed her to save significantly more than if she were shelling out $2,000 in rent. Even if she and her friends decided to share an apartment, the overall expenses would still be too high for their budgets. A few weeks later, Aleena and her friends went to the Comic-Con.

“Wow, I can’t believe we’re here,” Tiki giggled, she’s clearly giddy over the trip.

“Do you think we’ll see anyone famous here?” Liz asked, as her eye greenish brown almond shaped eyes scan the large room, filled with people.

“I’m sure we will, let’s check out the booths,” Aleena said. The trio enjoyed themselves and met like-minded individuals. As the day started to wind down, Aleena and her friends decided to hit a McDonald’s close by. “Once we’re back, I really want to check out that booth and grab some handmade Doctor Who magnets,” Liz mentioned. She’s been a huge fan of the show for ages, especially when it comes to David Tennant. Aleena said, "Sure, but I need to head back to the hotel to change into my jeans and a long-sleeved shirt."

"Same here," Tiki added. Liz replied, a bit let down,

"Alright then." The three of them returned to the hotel room to switch into their evening outfits. Aleena opted for a white button-up shirt, an olive suede vest, and jeans. Liz sported a red denim jacket, a white tee, and black jeans and Tiki threw on her teal green sweater and a pair of jeans. Liz was in the bathroom, brushing her long dark blonde hair and applying some peachy lipstick. Tiki knocked on the door and asked, "Are you almost done?" She really needed to use the bathroom.

Liz sighed dramatically and said, "yesss."

She walked out as Tiki hurried inside. Tikki also readied herself, fluffing up her curly black hair, she powdered her mocha-colored skin and checked her eyeliner. After checking out her reflection, she gave herself a nod and walked out.

Eventually, the trio made their way back to Comic-Con. As they strolled through the bustling aisles, exploring booths and soaking in the atmosphere, Liz suddenly froze.

"No way," she silently exclaimed, gesturing toward a room where a Doctor Who panel is, and likely David Tennant was there. They walked in and she saw him sitting alongside fellow actors. She gazed at Aleena, her eyes sparkling with excitement, and Aleena playfully rolled her eyes before giving a nod.

"Alright, let's do this." They settled into seats at the back, but Liz was unfazed; all she wanted was to catch a glimpse of David Tennant. "Tiki, I need to hit the restroom. I'll be right back," Aleena said, making

her way out. Tiki acknowledged her with a nod before refocusing on the panel. After 45 minutes had passed, Liz and Tiki exited the room and started looking for Aleena. "Do you think she could be back at the hotel?" Tiki asked, scanning the area.

"I'll give her a call," Liz replied, but there was silence on the other end. Tiki sent a text to Aleena, but it didn't go through, leaving them both exchanging worried glances.

A frown creased Liz's forehead as she shrugged and said, "I have no idea." They paused and leaned against a wall, scanning the crowd of people, but Aleena was nowhere in sight.

Tiki suggested, "Perhaps she went back to the Doctor Who panel room. She might've thought we were still there."

Liz looked confused, "It's hard to believe she'd just vanish, so she must be nearby. We'll need to search for her," she said, taking Tiki's hand. "Let's get moving."

They wandered through the convention room, checking nearly every corner before making their way to the restrooms. Tiki remarked, "I doubt she's still around here." After searching the restroom without success, they were heading out when they almost collided with *Eli Marsh.* He was clad in a sharp black blazer and jeans, his dark hair neatly slicked back. Liz's voice faded as she recognized him. "Oh my gosh," she exclaimed, her breath catching. *"It's Eli Marsh, the wealthiest man on the planet!"* She mused, as she glanced over at Tiki, who mirrored her astonishment with wide eyes. Liz's voice faded as she recognized him. "Pardon me, ladies," he said with a

charming smile as he made his way to the restrooms, with a bodyguard trailing behind him. “He must be his bodyguard," Tiki murmured as they observed him vanish around the corner. They resumed their search through the crowd of people, eager to locate Aleena.

2

Who's That Girl?

Aleena suddenly realized she was not at the Comic-Con. The walls were adorned with old yellow, peeling wallpaper, the incessant hum of the fluorescent lights overhead filled her ears, and a peculiar odor wafted into her nostrils.

"Where am I?" she wondered aloud, standing in the middle of a room with corridors branching off in various directions. She took a moment and glanced around. Her hazel eyes growing wide with apprehension. Memories flooded back—she had been in the restroom, and after stepping out, she was heading down a hallway back toward the Con when something caught her attention: a *peculiar yellow door.* A vivid glow streamed through the gap in the door. Overcome by curiosity, she pushed it open. As she entered, a wave of energy surged through her, causing her knees to give way, and she collapsed onto the floor. The room seemed to whirl around her, and when she finally blinked her eyes open, she found herself staring at a worn, yellowish carpet that looked like it had seen better days. She shook her head, regretting her decision to have opened that door. Glancing around, she muttered, "What the Hell is this place?" Rising to her feet, she took a few cautious steps, her heart racing. "If I just keep moving, maybe I'll stumble upon the door I came in from," she

reassured herself. She kept walking and walking, but everywhere she looked, it was just more of the same—yellow rooms and hallways. No matter which way she turned, she ended up in the same spots. It felt like she was stuck in a maze. A wave of fear and anxiety washed over her, making it feel like she had walked straight into a nightmare. The only noise was the buzzing of the fluorescent lights overhead, which flickered occasionally, leaving her curious about what was going on.

"There's light here, so there's electricity, but it feels like this place is," she hesitated, "completely empty of other people," she said to herself. Taking her phone from her clutch, she checked for signal bars.

"No signal at all," she murmured, frustration evident in her sigh as she tucked the phone back and tightened her grip on the clutch strap, moving forward.

She paused at a wall marked with the words, ***"The Peasant Girl,"*** contemplating the message.

"Someone must have written this," she thought.

Continuing down the hallway, she noticed an arrow that appeared to be painted red. As she got closer, her heart raced when she realized it was blood, not paint, prompting a soft gasp and a step back. With wide eyes, she scanned her surroundings, convinced she heard an eerie sound in the distance.

3

Eli Marsh

Eli Marsh stood at the sink, scrubbing his hands as he directed his guard to find his son and girlfriend mingling where the booths were at the Comic Con. Commitment was never Eli's strong suit; he shied away from the responsibilities of a devoted husband but despite having had four wives and a multitude of children, his vast fortune enabled him to shower his kids with extravagant gifts and a lifestyle that many could only fantasize about.
His bodyguard looked at him with a furrowed brow, "Are you really going to be okay, sir?"
Eli flashed a smirk and replied, "Yessss," rolling his eyes for emphasis.
"I'll just put on my sunglasses, and nobody will recognize me," he joked. The bodyguard sighed, shaking his head as he stepped out of the restroom.
Eli finished washing his hands, looking at his reflection in the restroom mirror, he donned a black baseball cap and slid on his sunglasses before stepping outside. He looked sharp in his sleek black blazer, a fitted white button-up shirt, and denim jeans. After a moment's thought, he removed his cap and placed it on a nearby trash bin. He chuckled to himself, pondering how wearing a cap seemed a bit excessive. His shades had a soft brown tint to them, giving people a sneak peek at his gorgeous, alluring

hazel eyes. As he strolled down the hallway, something caught his attention—a peculiar yellow door that stood out. There was something captivating about it, as if it were inviting him, urging him to open it. He felt a tingling sensation at the nape of his neck, a shiver coursing through him. An extraordinary moment was on the horizon, one that would alter the course of his life forever. *Curiosity kills the cat.* When he swung the door open, he stumbled and found himself face down on a carpeted floor. *"What just happened?"* he wondered, feeling slightly disoriented as he pushed himself upright. Rubbing his eyes, he spotted his sunglasses nearby and glanced around, realizing he was in an oddly unsettling yellow room that felt liminal in some way.

"Hello?" he shouted, but the silence was deafening. Swallowing hard, he began to walk, each turn revealing yet another room that mirrored the last. "Is anyone here?" he called out, his voice trailing off into the stillness. The incessant hum of the fluorescent lights above added to his unease, and a frown creased his brow. As he wandered through the labyrinth of vacant rooms and corridors, it occurred to him that this might be an odd Halloween maze, perhaps designed for a party and yet not quite finished. But the absence of typical festive figures and the fact that it was far from Halloween left him puzzled about the true nature of the place. "Can someone help me?" he yelled again, his voice tinged with desperation. Standing in the middle of a spacious room with his hands on his hips, frustration was evident on his face as he let out a deep sigh. Just then, he heard a noise that didn't sound human.

Taking a deep breath, he chose to move away from the sound, quickening his pace as a chilling screech echoed behind him. He dashed down a corridor and entered another vast, empty room. He noticed a message hastily painted in red on the wall: "Exit," accompanied by an arrow indicating the way. Compelled by curiosity, he chose to pursue it. The building's non-Euclidean architecture sent a shiver down his spine; everything felt unsettlingly askew.

4

Which Way?

Aleena's legs feel as though they are weighed down by lead, and the fatigue is dragging her further down. She knows that if she stops, even for a moment, the maze will change, potentially leading her to a place she dreads. With a resigned breath, she continues her journey.

"Where am I?" she pondered aloud. As she turned another corner, she found herself in a hallway that revealed an extraordinary sight.

"This can't be real," she whispered, her gaze fixed on a pool situated right in the center of the corridor. As she navigated the perplexing non-Euclidean maze, its very presence left her questioning its purpose. The hallway stretched endlessly before her, and when she glanced back, she was taken aback by the shifting walls that altered her surroundings.

"What the hell," she whispered, contemplating her options to either forge ahead or retreat. Opting to go back, she turned a corner and unexpectedly entered a grand room filled with towering columns, the maze itself a riddle. With a heavy sigh, she admitted, "I have no idea where I'm going." After what felt like an interminable journey, she spotted a wooden crate in the distance, its lid slightly ajar and with considerable effort, she managed to open it.

As it fell to the side, an unsettling feeling washed over her, as if unseen eyes are watching. She peered into the crate and discovered a collection of bottles. *"Almond water,"* she mused, examining the liquid as she grasped the bottle, a label on it reading good for you. The bottle was reminiscent of a Snapple tea bottle, featuring a

straightforward front label that read *"almond water,"* with no details on the back. She reflected on her growing thirst.

"Well, here goes nothing," she remarked as she unscrewed the cap. The liquid flowed smoothly down her throat and its gentle sweetness delightful. She felt lucky that peanuts didn't trigger her allergies; otherwise, she would be in a dangerous situation. After finishing the bottle, she decided to pick up another for her journey. Following a brief pause, she continued navigating the seemingly endless maze, hoping that she would find someone who can help her. Aleena trudges through the foreboding maze, each step feeling heavier than the last as exhaustion begins to take its toll. Her supply of almond water is running dangerously low, leaving her parched and desperate for hydration. The gnawing hunger in her stomach is a constant reminder of her dwindling resources, making her acutely aware of her need for sustenance. In this surreal and nightmarish landscape, the absence of mirrors adds to her unease; she can only *imagine* how her reflection might look.

She suspects that her face has taken on a haggard appearance, etched with fatigue, and she fears that she has lost weight, her body becoming a mere shadow of its former self. The combination of physical depletion and psychological strain weighs heavily on her, amplifying her sense of isolation in this labyrinthine nightmare.

Eventually, she came across a room featuring a tiny kitchen, tucked away in a corner. As she drew closer, she scrutinized the counter and sink with a wary gaze, noting every detail. The surfaces were a mix of yellow and white. Her attention was caught by the steady drip of water from the faucet. Although she felt a strong urge to take a sip, her instincts warned her that it could be a dangerous choice. She rummaged through the cupboards and discovered a single box of energy bars. The label read: ***Good for You***.

"What?" she murmured under her breath. She ripped open the packaging and took a tiny bite. To her surprise, it had the same flavor as an ordinary energy bar. Once she finished the whole bar, a wave of energy washed over her. She thought to herself, *"Wow, I'm not tired anymore,"* as she grabbed three energy bars. With renewed energy, she kept walking, looking for the exit. It hit her that she would eventually need something to carry items that she might find along the way. She moved cautiously through the yellow rooms and corridors, heading towards a door. When she opened it, she stepped into an office that was largely unoccupied. Unlike the yellow area that had enveloped her before, this space resembled typical offices, but they were all empty.

In one of them, she discovered a black and white backpack. Inside, she found a sizable knife with a dry peculiar residue on the blade and a neatly folded piece of paper. With care, she unfolded it and began to read.

To whom it may concern, may the contents in this backpack serve you well. Follow the exits but don't open the red door. Stay safe and may God be with you. Aleena swallowed hard, pondering the fate of the backpack's owner. She grabbed the energy bars and tucked them inside. With firm motion, she slung the backpack over her shoulder and pressed on with her exploration of the office. As she rounded a corner, she noticed the words *"The Backrooms"* hastily scrawled on the wall in red spray paint. "What are the Backrooms?" she mused, a sense of confusion washing over her. As she surveyed her surroundings, an unsettling and ominous feeling began to settle in.

"Where am I?" she whispered to herself.

5

Aleena's Plight

Aleena roamed through the maze for what felt like days, navigating its twists and turns with no end in sight. She was incredibly thankful for the backpack she found, as it offered a place to store any essentials she might come across. Along the way, she discovered another crate filled with almond water, but unfortunately, there were no energy bars to be found. With a deep breath, she pressed on, feeling the weight of her surroundings. She suspected that the food she had discovered could be her sole sustenance in this nightmarish Hell. As she moved forward, she noticed a door that stood out, lacking the usual neon red "**Exit**" sign above it. Taking a moment to gather herself, she prepared to approach it.

"Should I go in?" she pondered. After a moment of contemplation, she nodded to herself, setting her backpack down at her feet. She unzipped it and pulled out the knife. It is a substantial blade, and although the handle showed signs of wear, it remained a formidable weapon. Earlier, she had heard something eerie, and unnatural. Deep down, she understood that any noise she makes would likely draw whatever it was toward her. She isn't hesitant to wield a knife, but she often wishes she owned a handgun. Her father, a military veteran, taught her the basics of using a

firearm, yet she has always been reluctant to purchase one for her own safety. She swung the door open and stepped into a sprawling, vacant warehouse. It was a chilly and musty environment. The atmosphere of her new environment sent a wave of unease through her. She turned quickly, only to discover that the door had vanished. This revelation didn't shock her; she had encountered similar strange happenings before in the yellow maze. She pondered, *"I wonder if this place will change and shift as well,"* recalling how the walls in the yellow labyrinth would transform. She moved a few steps ahead, her heart pounding and fear evident in her eyes. With a tight grip on the knife, she pushed further into the eerie environment that awaited her. She observed a peculiar mist hovering near the concrete floor of the vast, empty space, unsure if it was a warehouse or an underground parking lot, perhaps it was a mix of both. As she moved forward, a foul odor filled the air, and a chill wrapped around her. She regrets not bringing a jacket or something similar.

"As if I could have predicted I'd end up here," she chuckled quietly to herself. Odd, dark puddles are dotted around the place. She paused a short distance from one of them. She pondered, *"I wonder if that water is real,"* and stepped a bit closer. While gazing into the puddle, a grey, claw-like hand suddenly shot out and grabbed her hair. Startled, she screamed and lunged at the hand with her knife. A loud wail echoed

from deep within the puddle. The monstrous hand released her hair, and she quickly sprang to her feet, dashing away in the opposite direction. A quick look over her shoulder revealed a terrifying creature, towering at around 7 feet with grey, grotesque skin, relentlessly pursuing her. It seemed to have emerged from the puddle—or perhaps it was the puddle itself, transformed into this nightmarish being that was now in fierce pursuit. Dashing from one area to another and racing down the hallways, Aleena felt her hope dwindling. Her heart pounded in her chest, and as she veered into yet another corridor, she looked back to find that the creature had mysteriously stopped chasing her. She eased her pace until she finally halted. Leaning against the concrete wall, tears began to roll down her face.

"No, I won't give up," she gasped for air.

"I will find a way out." She continued onward and spotted three wooden crates—two piled on top of each other and one positioned beside them. Hurrying over, she attempted to lift the lid of one crate. It suddenly toppled open, causing her to gasp as she quickly glanced around, anxious that another Eldritch creature might have been alerted by the noise. She rummaged through the crate and discovered three bottles of almond water and two energy bars. At the bottom, she came across a white T-shirt, stained and it smelled a bit, but it is still usable, along with an olive-green Bomber jacket that has a pin at the front. The jacket is a bit dirty, yet acceptable to wear. She put on the jacket and shoved the t-shirt into her backpack. With a heavy sigh, she pressed on. After what felt like an eternity of roaming through the

hallways and stark concrete rooms, she stumbled upon a corridor lined with metal doors and tried to open them a few times but to no avail. The doors were painted a bright blue and as she walked down the lengthy hallway, she spotted puddles here and there.

She stopped for a second, her forehead creased with concern, a worried expression crossing her face as she let out a sigh. She looked up and noticed some water dripping from the ceiling.

"I have to tread lightly," she mused. As she moved with caution, she noticed a door that was slightly ajar. Out of nowhere, a low, menacing growl emanated from behind it, causing her to freeze in place. Her heart pounded in her chest, beads of sweat formed on her brow, and she gripped the knife tightly in her hand. A strange and grotesque creature gradually emerged from behind the door, its pale white eyes glinting beneath tangled hair. She instinctively stepped back, her heart racing as the creature came fully into view and a gasp escaped her lips. Her eyes widened in disbelief as she took in its Eldritch Horror form. It bore a striking resemblance to a dog, but its elongated snout and unsettlingly human-like features gave it an eerie presence that was hard to shake off. The creature's thick, matted black fur hung in disarray, obscuring much of its face and adding to its menacing aura. Its limbs, though slender, exuded a sense of latent power, each ending in sharp, claw-like appendages that hinted at a predatory nature. The combination of its wild appearance and those unsettling pale grey eyes made it a terrifying sight to behold.

The creature appeared ghostly white, its claws reminiscent of a werewolf. As it approached her, it crawled in a way that imitated a human, but its hind legs were bent, giving it a distinctly canine look. Its empty gaze makes it seem blind, but she has a feeling it can see just fine. The rows of sharp teeth adorned its large maw. When it opened it, a strange hiss sounded, it was then when Aleena dashed away, but the otherworldly beast was right on her heels. Terror gripped her as she heard its heavy footsteps thundering just behind her. Despite wielding a knife, she sensed that it wouldn't be enough to bring it down. Each breath felt like it could be her final one. As she rounded a corner, she spotted graffiti on the wall that read, "**Find Him**."

"I can't afford to waste time thinking; I need to locate a door quickly," she thought to herself. Her excitement surged as she spotted a door marked with the word **Exit.** Eager for it to truly be an escape, she quickened her pace and nearly collided with the door. To her relief, she swung it open and swiftly shut it behind her. Her heart raced wildly in her chest.

"Wow," she murmured. As she glanced around, she realized she was in a completely different location. Pipes were releasing steam, and the air felt warm. She got to her feet slowly and turned to find that the door had disappeared, replaced by a solid wall. She removed her jacket and shoved it into her backpack. As she navigated the seemingly endless underground tunnels lined with rusty pipes, hot steam billowed out from them, she rubbed her eyes, smudging her makeup in the process. Pausing for a moment, she placed her backpack on the ground.

"It's too hot," she remarked and unbuttoned her shirt, removed it, and used her knife to tear off the sleeves. The result was a makeshift sleeveless top that had a slightly rough appearance. Up to this point, she hasn't encountered any creatures, but from afar, she hears a scratching sound followed by an eerie moan. With a furrowed brow, she contemplates what other beings might be lurking nearby. Continuing onward, she picks up her pace to a trot, carefully sidestepping the steam billowing from the pipes. Aleena feels the pangs of hunger creeping in, and while she has two bottles of almond water stashed in her backpack, she's reluctant to drink them too quickly. She knows she needs to locate more supplies soon. *"This is Hell,"* she thought to herself. As she rounded a corner, she spotted a message scrawled in red spray paint: "**Run**!" Without a second thought, she glanced back and saw a long-armed, grey-skinned creature sprinting toward her. With its razor-sharp claws and a wide mouth brimming with jagged teeth, it was a terrifying sight. She let out a scream and sprinted away with all her might.

6

Into the Suburbs

Aleena has made her way through various levels of the Backrooms and has now found herself in a strangely familiar suburban neighborhood. She can't recall how she got there, but she vividly remembers being pursued by one of those terrifying Eldritch Horror creatures. She quietly pondered, *"I wonder if anyone else is here. It seems oddly quiet.*" Pausing for a moment, she strained to hear, convinced she detected footsteps echoing in the distance. As she turned, she narrowed her eyes and peered down the street, searching for any hint of activity. She was alone, but her experiences at previous levels had put her on high alert. The challenges she faced in those places had significantly eroded her trust in others. One location featured a labyrinth of tunnels constructed from bricks and cement, with each room housing an electrical device that Aleena believes powers the other levels she has navigated through. Additionally, there was a maze of deserted offices, filled only with emptiness, yet within it lurked another strange entity. Lurking behind the windows, the entity is ready to snatch up anyone naive enough to believe they can escape by opening the windows. She saw through its trickery and steered clear of the windows. Then there was the ominous hotel, filled with its own set of bizarreness.

The death moths were challenging, yet she successfully evaded them as she flung open a door and dashed through. The scenery transformed, and she suddenly found herself on a quiet neighborhood street. *"Where am I now?"* she wondered, inhaling deeply. The night air was refreshing and brisk, and with each step, her feet crunched over the brittle leaves scattered on the ground. The asphalt beneath her is worn and fractured. Aleena moved forward carefully, gripping the knife tightly in her hand. Her eyes were wide and vigilant. She donned the olive-green bomber jacket she had discovered earlier. The white blouse she had been wearing was ripped in multiple spots, so she opted for a slightly damaged white T-shirt she had found instead. It has been days since her last shower, and she probably wouldn't get the chance to clean up unless she stumbled upon a secure location with running water. She has several bruises on her arms and one on her cheek, but fortunately, none are severe. She accidentally made a deep cut on herself. To control the bleeding, she ripped a piece from an old shirt and wrapped it around her arm just above the wrist, as the blood was starting to attract attention. After sipping the almond water, she noticed about an hour later that the bleeding had stopped. When she took off the bandage, she discovered that the cut had healed.

"Wow, oh my god, this is amazing," she muttered. It intrigued her, but she didn't dwell on it. She viewed it as a quiet blessing. She discovered a note tucked away in a desk of the office maze, which said: *don't drink the water unless it's almond water.* Although she wasn't entirely sure what it meant, she decided to

follow the advice. As she moved along, she wished to find something to munch on. The almond water was getting low too. She thinks that every level has a knack for crafting situations that force travelers into tough choices between life and death.

"Day or night," she said, taking a moment to breathe. "How can anyone really tell what time it is here?" Even though it feels like night where she is, she's fully aware that every location she's been to has its own set of eerie challenges ready for the next visitor. She fears that this level is no different. She carefully steps into one of the houses. She thought about calling out to see if anyone was hiding inside but chose not to, fully aware that making any noise could lead to a deadly encounter with some unexpected creature lurking within. She glanced around the living room before heading into the kitchen. The space was a bit messy, but not overly dirty. When she opened the fridge, she discovered it was completely bare. *"What do I expect?"* she thought to herself as she kept searching through the house. Then, she stumbled upon something unusual. In a room on the house's lower level, she discovered a dagger in its sheath. Next, she stumbled upon a flashlight and turned it on to check if it functioned. It did, but the light is weak. "Damn," she muttered quietly.

"Maybe there are batteries around here." She searched frantically but found nothing. Suddenly, she heard what sounded like chanting. A look of confusion flashed across her face. She sprinted out, leaving her backpack behind, but the dagger she had found was securely fastened to her belt. As she got closer, she saw a crowd gathered, cheering for a

picture that one of them was proudly displaying. She moved in a little closer and gave a timid smile. "Hello?" But they didn't see her, so she took a small step back. Their behavior seemed off. *"What's up with them?"* she wondered. Just then, a woman with long blonde hair and blue wide eyes, turned to look at her with a crazed look on her face.

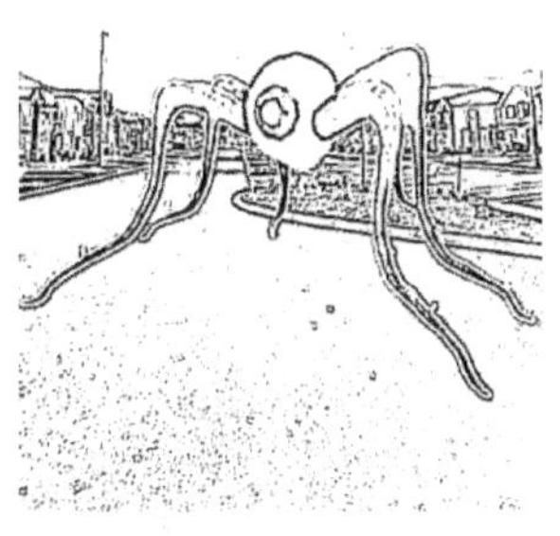

She held up an 11 by 14 picture of a blue parrot and exclaimed, "Praise our glorious God, our savior Polly!" Aleena slowly backed away, her heart racing.

"Something's wrong with these people," she mused. From a distance, she spotted two horrifying creatures sprinting in their direction. Her eyes grew wide with terror as she dashed back to the house where she had left her backpack. She locked the door and took refuge behind a curtain, peeking through a narrow gap to observe the approaching creatures. As they got closer, she noticed their unusual shape. They resembled a giant eye supported by optic nerves that twisted into spider-like legs. It was a sight straight out of a nightmare, and they could move with astonishing speed. She felt an urge to scream at the crowd in the street, but she feared that doing so would reveal her location, prompting the creatures to pursue her also. From her vantage point, she witnessed the horrifying scene as those monsters decimated some individuals while the rest fled in panic. One of those creatures was pursuing the ones that had fled, while the

remaining one scanned the street with its large eye. She inhaled deeply and cautiously ascended the stairs, her hand resting on the dagger's sheath. She had left her backpack on the couch. As she peered into each room, she discovered nothing of significance. Suddenly she heard a noise. Gingerly, she made her way to a room with a closed door. A floorboard let out a soft creak beneath her feet. Pausing, she held her breath and twisted the doorknob. As she pushed the door open, she spotted a man sprawled out on a twin bed. Glancing around, she realized it was a child's room. She approached him and took a position next to him, gripping the dagger tightly looking down, curious about his identity.

"How can anyone possibly sleep here?" she wondered. Pulling up a chair beside the bed, she settled in, her gaze fixed on him, debating whether to rouse him. *"How could he have slept through the screams from outside? He must be completely worn out,"* she thought. As she gazed at him, he seemed oddly familiar to her. He shifted to his side unexpectedly, and she hoped he would awaken, but he remained asleep. Gently, she touched his forehead. *"He feels warm. I wonder if he has a fever,"* she pondered. Recalling the almond water she had packed; she quietly made her way downstairs to retrieve it. The vast, dark night outside filled her with dread.

7

The Man in the Bed

"I'm not sure dawn is ever going to arrive," she murmured, concern etched on her face. She picked up her backpack and headed upstairs. As she stepped into the room, she saw him gradually waking up.

"Hey," she said gently, catching him off guard. He sat up and asked, "Who are you?" His voice was faint and filled with apprehension. She paused for a moment, let out a sigh, and said, "I'm not one of those crazy people, so don't worry."

He propped himself up and looked at her intently. She settled into the chair beside the bed and rummaged through her backpack, pulling out a half-full bottle of almond water. That was the last of her almond water stash. He hesitated for a moment when she handed him the water bottle but eventually took it from her. After a sip, he grimaced and asked, "What is this?"

"It's almond water; it should make you feel better," she replied. He rolled his eyes and finished it off, leaving the bottle empty. Aleena, with her innate kindness, can't help but feel compassion for the stranger; she simply can't stand to see anyone in pain.

"Do you have any more?" he asked.

"Not enough, we need to look for more," she said softly.

He attempted to get up but felt a wave of dizziness. Aleena supported him until he steadied himself.

"We should get out of here," she proposed.

He agreed with a nod. They made their way downstairs and took a quick look out the window.

"It seems like it's clear for now, but I really think we should stay close," Aleena suggested. The man then asked, "How did you end up here?"

She replied, "I was at the Comic-Con when I stumbled upon this ordinary yellow door, and after stepping through, I found myself in a," she hesitated, recalling her journey through the terrifying yellow maze. "Let's just say I'm thankful to have made it this far."

He asked about the water, and she explained, "I discovered some bottles in a wooden crate." The dim light in the house, mostly from the fading streetlights, made it hard for her to see his face clearly, but once she does, she will recognize him. They cautiously stepped out of the front door. She mentioned that she had only encountered the terrifying one-eyed creatures wandering the streets, but she suspects there are even more horrible ones lurking around.

She told him about the odd creature that had tugged at her hair while she peered into a puddle, he listened intently. He then admitted he had never ventured into that level before, having only explored the yellow maze, and a brick-and-concrete labyrinth filled with electrical devices in the rooms before arriving here. Although she was curious to learn more about him, she decided to hold off on further questions until they were in a safer place, as an unsettling feeling crept over her, making her sense they were being watched.

"I can't help but wonder if that one-eyed thing is keeping an eye on us," she pondered aloud.
In the dim light, she caught a clearer glimpse of his face; he had a five o'clock shadow, pale skin likely from being sick, and was dressed in a black blazer and jeans. His hazel eyes radiated warmth, almost relieved to find someone to talk to amidst the madness of the suburbs. They continued walking down the street, the eerie silence occasionally broken by distant sounds of creatures, prompting them to dash away from the noise.

"This dreadful place seems to stretch on forever," he remarked.

"It's similar to the other levels, but I'm sure there's an exit somewhere," Aleena chimed in, taking a moment to catch her breath. She drew her dagger from its sheath, catching the man's attention.

"Where did you get that?" he asked.

"I found it, and it's quite useful. Without a weapon, it's much tougher to fight your way through," she replied. She had built a tough exterior, one that proved invaluable in the Backrooms. Without it, she wouldn't have made it as far as she had. He acknowledged her with a nod, and she returned his gesture with a smile as they pressed on. Out of nowhere, an unholy howl echoed from behind them, reminiscent of a wolf yet oddly tinged with human-like quality. As they turned, a horrifying creature that seemed to be a mix of human/wolf, almost looking like a werewolf, yet not quite, lunged at them. Aleena madly stabbed at it a few times with her dagger, kicking at it too, causing it to hesitate for a moment. Seizing the opportunity, the man fiercely kicked the

beast away and grabbed Aleena's hand, urging her to run. “It won’t be long before it catches up!” he yelled as they dashed toward a nearby house, slamming the door behind them. Leaning against the door, they suddenly felt a strange shift in reality. Their bodies spinning as they squeezed their eyes shut.

When they opened them again, they found themselves standing in a vast wheatfield, the door nowhere in sight. They tried to balance themselves as the ordeal made them feel dizzy. Staring at each other in disbelief, Aleena finally recognized him. *“Eli Marsh,”* she muttered, her voice filled with surprise.

8

Getting To Know You

Aleena was taken aback as she gazed at the face of a man who inspired both disdain and admiration. *"The wealthiest man on the planet,"* she thought, her forehead creased as she turned away. He caught her reaction but opted to remain silent, sensing that she recognized his identity.

"How did you end up in this nightmarish place?" she asked.

"I was at the Comic-Con with my wife and my kid when a simple trip to the restroom became the last thing I did before ending up here," he said, taking a moment to catch his breath. As they wandered through the wheatfields, a delicate scent of almond water floated in the air, wrapping around them like a warm embrace. Eli animatedly recounted the peculiar encounter he had with a yellow door. In turn, Aleena shared her own story in detail of how she found herself lost in the yellow discombobulated maze, her voice laced with intrigue. "It seems like fate brought us together," Eli remarked, a playful grin spreading across his face. Aleena couldn't help but smile softly, her gaze drifting over the endless expanse of swaying wheat. Aleena picked a stem and took a whiff before giving it a lick. To her surprise, the wheat had an almond scent and flavor. Puzzled, she remarked, "This is odd; it's meant to be wheat, but it smells and

tastes like almonds." Eli grabbed a stem and mimicked her actions. "Do you think this works like the almond water?" Aleena got what he was hinting at. "I'm still feeling under the weather," he added.

"I'm not sure, but this whole area has an almond scent," she replied. Eli gnawed at the wheat stem, wishing it would help him feel better. As they continued walking, she asked him, "How did you get sick?"

"I don't know but while I was in the yellow maze, I spotted a drinking fountain and took a sip from it." Aleena remembers the note she found and how it warned her not to drink the water. She then told Eli,

"This place has many ways to kill you, and all are permanent," she noted.

"Do you think I will die?" he asked. She shook her head and shrugged, "I'm not sure but when you drank the almond water, it made you feel better, right?" He nodded.

"We're just going to have to find more," Aleena said.

"We'll get through this together," he replied, gently grasping her hand. She gulped. *"I can't believe I'm here with Eli Marsh,"* she mused and shyly turned away. "May I ask your name?" he asked.

"I'm Aleena, Aleena Smart, and it seems we both have stepped through the same yellow door," she paused before adding, "By the way, I know who you are." He figured she recognized him. "I'm surprised you were at Comic-Con as well," she said.

"I wanted to go and take my kid with me. As for my wife, she just happened to tag along," he replied, his tone slightly detached.

Aleena sensed that he and his wife were going through some kind of marital issues. Her expression tightened as she contemplated whether the rumors about him were true.

"He's a womanizer, embodying all the traits that a gold-digger might find appealing, but I'm not like that. I'm not a dreamy-eyed girl who will be captivated by his charm and allure. My only desire is to find a way back home," she pondered. With a sense of resolve, she released his hand and came to a stop, her heart racing as she contemplated the journey ahead.

She remarked, "We should look for a road or something similar." He agreed with a nod. While they meandered through the wheatfields, Aleena observed puddles scattered along the path. Her brow furrowed, pondering their existence. She crouched down, reached out to touch it, and took a whiff.

"This is almond water," she remarked. Eli followed suit, kneeling to scoop some of the liquid into his palm before taking a sip. Aleena grimaced at the sight; she raised an eyebrow and chortled. Eli suddenly noticed a large, imposing creature. He nudged her shoulder and gestured toward it. Aleena gasped, whispering, "Wow." They took a step back, but the creature didn't pay them any mind; it wasn't bothered by their presence at all. Instead, it kept munching on the wheat and oozing some weird liquid from its skin, forming a puddle beneath it. Eli Marsh's face went white when he spotted the odd liquid, and he felt a wave of nausea wash over him. Aleena let out a soft laugh. "I suppose those puddles of almond water are from this creature," she teased.

"Please don't say that," Eli replied, struggling with his queasiness, while Aleena continued to find the situation entertaining. She remembers all the stories she heard about him on the news and is aware of his identity and his past actions. In fact, prior to his departure from politics, many speculated he would flee the country, yet who could have imagined he would find himself in this dreadful place? Who could've imagined that she would be in a place like that, with him. She harbors no affection for him and feels indifferent, but he is the only familiar face from her world that she has encountered in that godforsaken place. Eli continued to spit, attempting to rid his mouth of the lingering taste.

"Are you okay?" Aleena asked; her voice laced with mild amusement. Eli made a face and replied, "Yes." They pressed on, and as they strolled through the golden wheat fields, an unusual sense of tranquility washed over them. The aroma of almonds combined with the peculiar fluffy lavender sky and clouds overhead, created an enchanting atmosphere.

"Aleena, are you attending college?"

"Yes, but I'm currently on break until after summer." He smiled, paused, and glanced around, noticing a few gentle, ogre-like creatures grazing nearby. "They remind me of cows, just grazing," he remarked. Aleena agreed with a nod. "This place is quite strange," she said thoughtfully before asking, "Do

you feel a sense of unusual calmness?" He lifted an eyebrow at her inquiry and replied, "A bit, what makes you curious?"

"I believe it's the atmosphere here. It has a soothing quality that wraps around everyone who visits."

Eli contemplated this. "Then we should seek a different path and carry on with our journey." Aleena felt a strange fatigue, attributing it to her empty stomach, while Eli's growling belly echoed his own hunger pangs. They continued their journey, the vast wheatfields pressing heavily upon them. Fatigue began to set in, and just as they walked, a light drizzle began to fall.

"What is that scent?" Aleena wondered. As the drizzle turned into a downpour, she and Eli dashed down the path, but no shelter was in sight. Aleena felt a sense of defeat as she became drenched.

Eli glanced around and said, "We can't do anything about it. We're going to get soaked," clearly annoyed by the downpour. Aleena gazed at the lavender clouds, opened her mouth, and realized the rain tastes like almond water.

"Ah, that explains the weird smell; it's almond water," she mused. Her eyes flew open as she motioned for Eli to part his lips, allowing the raindrops to cascade down their throats.

"Wow, it's almond water," Eli exclaimed, a puzzled expression crossing his face. "Amazing," he added.

Aleena pulled the almost empty bottle from her backpack and collected some rainwater in it. Once it was about halfway filled, she offered it to Eli. It was clear that Eli was still feeling sick, so the Almond water would likely benefit him. Aleena experienced a

rush of energy flowing through her, after she drank some and it seemed Eli felt revitalized as well. He returned the bottle to her, and as he did, his fingers brushed against hers, his smile conveying a deep message. In that instant, she felt a whirlwind of emotions, aware of his identity and the unsettling rumors surrounding him.

“Um, we should move onward,” she suggested as she blushed. He gave a nod, and they pressed on through the golden wheatfields. The rain had ceased, leaving a gentle almond fragrance wafting in the breeze. Aleena found herself wondering about Eli Marsh's age. If only her phone were working, she could easily check his Wikipedia page, but unfortunately, the battery had long since died. She suspected his phone was in the same state. From afar, Eli noticed an unusual tower. He gestured towards it, and they headed in that direction. Upon arrival, the imposing structure loomed before them.

"What is that?" Aleena whispered.

"A tower of sorts, it looks like a medieval castle or something like that," he answered. Then he added, "Could be a lookout tower." They both gazed at it, puzzled.

"You could be onto something; it could be a surveillance tower, but who exactly is keeping an eye on things?" She glanced warily at the windows overhead. Eli proposed they enter the building. "I don't think that's a good idea," Aleena replied, sensing that something was off about the place. Eli gently grasped her hand, saying, "It's alright, let's explore a bit." Aleena felt her cheeks heat up, uncertain if she was ready to trust him with her safety.

The wooden door let out a soft creak as Eli carefully pushed it open. With the knife safely sheathed, she placed her other hand on it as they carefully entered. They encountered a lengthy staircase ascending to the tower's summit. As they ascended, Aleena would glance down from time to time, anxious that a creature might be lurking behind them.

Eli asked, "What's the matter?"

"I just want to avoid any unexpected surprises, if you catch my drift."

"Ah yes, those terrifying beings we've both faced since stepping into this bizarre world," he replied.

Just before they reached the summit, Aleena stopped.

"I can't help but wonder why this place feels so deserted," she remarked. Her voice echoed off the walls, and she was unaware that she might have raised her voice too much. "It's okay," he reassured her, though his words offered little comfort. Aleena frowned and let out a deep sigh. They made it to the top and looked around. They kind of thought they would see more of the same, endless wheat fields, but off in the distance, there was a dirt road and a farmhouse further down the road. He smiled at Aleena, "That's where we need to go," he said. As Aleena glanced around, she noticed peculiar goblin-like creatures advancing from a distance. Unlike the gentle creatures they had encountered earlier in the wheatfields, these were clearly different.

"Look," she exclaimed, indicating the approaching group. They quickly descended the staircase.

"I just hope we can escape before they get to the tower," she said, her voice tinged with fear.

Eli nodded in agreement, and they quickened their steps. Upon leaving the tower, they veered away from the cluster of creatures they had seen. They navigated down a trail, maintaining a safe distance from the group. However, out of nowhere, a creature lunged at them, knocking Eli to the ground. With greenish skin and piercing yellow eyes, it glared menacingly as it drove an arrow into Eli's shoulder. Aleena leaped onto the goblin's back and, with a quick motion, she cut its throat. It emitted a terrible scream that echoed, alerting the other goblins nearby. Spotting a crossbow that had fallen from the creature, she quickly snatched it up.

"Let's go," she said, pulling Eli to his feet.

"We need to get out of here," she insisted with urgency. She understood that taking down one of those creatures would make her a target but at the moment, escape was all she thought about. They made it to the road and kept running. Despite the pain from his wound, Eli pushed through the agony and forged ahead. Not sure if the creatures were pursuing them, they had no time to ponder or pause to check for any signs of being followed. After what felt like an endless run, the farmhouse finally appeared in the distance. "Look!" Aleena exclaimed, her heart racing with excitement. Thankfully, the almond water they had consumed earlier seemed to have given them the boost they needed. They both let out a deep sigh of relief. Aleena's face flushed with color, and she felt

nauseous from the intense run they did. In contrast, Eli threw up, and blood oozed from his injury. Once they were inside; Aleena secured the door.
She looked around the Livingroom, which was surprisingly decent given the circumstances. There was only a light layer of dust on the furniture, and while the faded yellow walls had cobwebs in the corners, the space felt manageable. An old, brownish-grey couch was pushed against the wall, and a matching loveseat was on the opposite side. In the center, a dirty white carpet lay beneath a yellow chair that added a splash of color to the otherwise drab setting. Eli plopped down on the couch, sneezing from the dust, and asked, “What now?” He rubbed his eyes, feeling fatigued, much like her.
"I'm going to take care of that wound," Aleena stated. She pulled out a bottle containing just the right amount of almond water and handed it to Eli, then she headed to the kitchen to look for a dish cloth. After finding one, she took her knife and cut it into three-inch strips before returning to the Livingroom.
"Could you roll up the sleeve?" she asked.
"I’ll do better," he said as he started to unbutton his shirt, revealing his chiseled physique. Aleena couldn't help but gaze at his toned body. He carelessly tossed the soiled shirt aside. Sitting there, he hoped she would catch his gaze, but she was too focused on tending to his wound. He finds her modesty and quiet demeanor incredibly appealing. She rose to her feet, making her way to the kitchen to wash her hands. The water had an unpleasant odor, but since she didn't plan to drink it, she deemed it acceptable. Still, a sense of unease lingered within her about the water in

this strange and harsh environment. She re- entered the room. "Do you think we could take a shower?" Eli asked, and Aleena glanced at him, puzzled by his words.

"Together?" she asked, feeling a bit foolish for her question, yet intrigued by the possibility, as she sensed his attraction toward her, leaving her uncertain about his true intentions. He laughed and replied, "Only if we become more familiar with one another." She chuckled nervously, realizing that his inquiry was straightforward and simply referred to taking a shower alone. With a hint of embarrassment in her voice she said, "Well, I don't think that's a great idea." She sniffed her hands and noticed the weird smell still lingering. Sighing, she continued, "There's definitely something off about the water, so I think we should use it as little as possible."

He nodded in agreement, saying, "Alright, let's stay here for a few hours while we figure out if we should carry on with our journey or..."

“Yeah, I know," she interrupted, "We can't be sure if those goblins will pursue us or not." After a moment, she noticed he was still without a shirt, then said, “Maybe I should find a shirt for you. It’s possible there might be clothes here.” He nodded in agreement as he scanned her appearance. He admires the beauty before him, feeling a strong desire to connect with her on a deeper level, maybe even have sex with her. However, he hesitated to flirt, knowing he doesn’t know her well. *“Maybe later,”* he thought. Aleena ascended the stairs, she unsheathed her knife, catching Eli's attention. He regarded her with intrigue, thinking, *“Interesting girl, I think I like her.”*

While her primary goal was to find a way back home, a nagging worry crept in, the deeper they ventured into this enigmatic realm, the further she drifted away from going home. She pondered the potential awkwardness of being stuck with Eli, a thought that made her uneasy.

Although she had never considered him romantically, the prospect of developing a close bond as they spend more time together--unsettles her, especially given her history of feeling awkward around men and Eli's questionable past. As she rummaged through the vacant rooms, her search led her to a closet in the last room, where she discovered three men's button-up shirts. Grabbing a blue shirt, she made her way back downstairs and tossed it to Eli, who promptly slipped it on. As it started to rain again, they found themselves sitting quietly on the couch. Eli finally broke the silence, asking, "If you don't mind me asking, how old are you?" Aleena paused before answering, "I'm 21." Curious, she asked, "And how old are you?" With a playful smirk, he replied, "I'm 30," he lied. Aleena smiled softly, sensing he might be older, but it didn't really matter; they were both trapped in this hellish situation and needed to find a way to endure it together. They started sharing stories about their lives before arriving at their current situation. She discovered that he had dreams of leaving the States but felt anchored by his wife and son, although he mentioned they were contemplating a divorce. "I was going to attend the local community college but then this happened," she said. Noticing the worry etched on her face, he gently wrapped his arm around her in a comforting gesture. She didn't

pull away but remained cautious about the attention he was giving her. “We should sleep but should we take turns or…” Aleena started. Eli suggested they take turns, expressing his willingness to share the watch. “With this intriguing crossbow and your knife, I feel confident that we can manage.” She agreed with a nod, and he allowed her to rest first.

As he observed Aleena sleeping peacefully, he quietly rose from his seat and gazed out the window. The night was absent, replaced by an eerie mix of rain and fog that shifted back to rain.

“It doesn’t seem to ever become nighttime here,” he mused. During their time outside, they had noticed peculiar clouds looming overhead. The rain was almond water, and Eli pondered the seemingly endless fields around them. Having discovered one house, he held onto a glimmer of hope that more would be found, and perhaps, they might even encounter other people.

9

Infinite Grocery Store

Eli and Aleena pressed on along the dusty path, which appeared to go on forever in both directions. Eli caught sight of the worried expression on Aleena's face. "Don't fret, we'll discover a way out of this place."

Aleena replied, "Yet here we are, navigating another section of this intricate dimension. It seems we've wandered into a realm that challenges all rational thought. This place is unlike the previous levels, but it may be just as perilous. I sincerely hope we don't encounter those goblins again."

Eli nodded, remarking, "This place feels like it's in a perpetually afternoon time zone." Aleena let out a scoff, followed by a light chuckle. "Exactly, and we have almond water to enjoy." Just then, raindrops started to fall, prompting Aleena to pull out the bottle and catch the rain, filling it up. They both took a sip together. As the rain eased, the sky transformed into a canvas of grey and lavender hues, enveloped by the fragrant aroma of almonds and wheat. Sipping the refreshing almond water revitalized them for the journey ahead. Eventually, they stumbled upon yet another farmhouse. They exchanged glances and dashed toward it. Cautiously entering, they found the interior in an even worse condition than the previous

place. The room was devoid of furniture, with curtains dangling from broken rods, and cobwebs and dust blanketing every surface of the ceiling walls. Aleena was eager to leave quickly. As they wandered through the house, they opened the door and unexpectedly stepped into a sprawling grocery store. Just as they decided to retreat, the door disappeared behind them. They exchanged a wary glance before continuing their exploration of the expansive grocery store, filled with row after row of food and, strangely, an abundance of what appeared to be water bottles. She unscrewed the cap of one and took a careful sip. It was only almond water but at least it was something. There appeared to be some soft drinks too. She opened one of them and took a sip. She made a face.

"Oh God, no way." She left it on the shelf. Eli looked at her, and she said, "I suppose almond water is in the abundance here but that soda, I wouldn't touch."

"Oh my God, just look at this! We have actual food! He exclaimed, and they embraced. The moment was uncomfortable yet unexpected when he kissed her, causing her cheeks to redden. She took a step back, letting out a nervous laugh. To shift the mood, she suggested they look for some food to take along. As she browsed the aisles, Eli did the same. "How about we grab a few bags of popcorn?" he shouted from

a couple of aisles away. Her eyes widened in surprise, and she hurried over to him. "Shh, keep your voice down," she urged, her tone filled with urgency.
"Why?" he murmured.
"Because in every place we've been to," she hesitated before continuing, "there's always something that..."
He interjected, "That could kill us, you're right and if it hears us, we're dead," he agreed and wrapped his arm around her shoulders.
"He's getting a bit too cozy with touching me," she thought. She looked away shyly and remarked, "We need to be careful here..." Her voice trailed off as she spotted a woman watching them from a short distance. Eli quickly turned and called out, "Hey, wait up!" The woman took off running down one of the aisles, while Aleena positioned herself at the other end to intercept her. The woman had messy, shoulder-length dark blonde hair, and her greenish-brown eyes were wide with fear and apprehension.
"Hold on, we just want to chat with you," Aleena said. The woman brandished a knife, making Aleena leap back. Eli caught up and asked the woman, "Who are you? Did you end up in this nightmarish place like we did?" A sudden voice broke the tension from behind Aleena.
"Leave her," a man ordered, leveling a pistol at them. His tousled light brown hair matched the intensity of his stern expression, which conveyed a clear message. Aleena cautiously stepped back and stood beside Eli with her hands raised. She shot a worried glance at Eli. Then she mustered the courage to say, "We're sorry if we have done something wrong," she

hesitated. "It's just that we haven't encountered anyone else in this strange, twisted dimension, and when we spotted her, we felt both excited and anxious about the possibility of another person being here." The man nodded in agreement. His stern eyes never wavered away from them. He slowly brought down his pistol and stared at them warily. Aleena scrutinized their attire with interest. He wore a, weathered brown leather jacket over a black t-shirt, and weathered faded jeans. There is a weapons holster strapped around his waist and he wore brown leather flat work boots, that have seen better days.

The woman beside him wore a faded denim jacket that bore the marks of time, paired with a blue T-shirt that had seen better days and equally distressed jeans, all complemented by flat leather boots that hinted at countless miles traveled. Aleena found herself intrigued, pondering the origins of their attire.

"This nightmarish dimension is known as the *Backrooms,*" the man revealed, his voice steady yet laced with an unsettling gravity.

"The Backrooms," Aleena echoed softly, the name hanging in the air like a dark omen. Eli, caught in the web of confusion, repeated, "The Backrooms?" as if trying to grasp the weight of the words. The man continued, "This twisted dimension, as you call it, is indeed the Backrooms. It consists of numerous levels, each presenting its own unique and perilous threats."

The woman interjected, her tone matter of fact, "You can bet on that." With a slight nod, she introduced herself, "My name is Syra, and this is Kyle," gesturing to the man beside her. Aleena and Eli reached out to greet Kyle, their hands met in a firm shake, a gesture that bridged the gap between strangers and allies. In that moment, Kyle, with a practiced motion, holstered his pistol, the weight of the weapon slipping away as he exhaled a deep, weary sigh.

"Well, you should come with us, we are a part of a colony, not the main factions but one of the smaller colonies. We have a place to stay, clothes, showers," he said.

"As you probably have figured out that the water in this place is almond water. Of course you're gonna smell a little like almonds," Syra said, with a chuckle. Aleena and Eli glanced at each other.

"Okay, show us the way," Eli said.

10

The Colony

Eli Marsh and Aleena completely lost track of time while they mingled with the locals. When they first arrived, Aleena noticed that the residents had constructed a wall around the community using metal sheets, bricks and wood. The metal sheets, standing tall at heights between 10 and 25 feet, looked like the kind used for aluminum roofing. They were supported by robust wooden poles anchored deep into the ground, with large stones stacked in front to enhance their stability.

Despite their rusty and weathered appearance, they effectively formed a fortress-like barrier. The fortress had an outer ring, and then there was an inner ring. Before anyone can enter the community, they'll have to get past the outer ring. Aleena noticed several towers, where there appeared to be someone standing watch. She asked if they had ever faced any creatures trying to break in.

Syra answered, "Yes, but our defenses have been strong enough to keep them away. We do get raiders sometimes, and we've dealt with them, even kill one or two if things get out of hand."

"Wow," Aleena mused. Syra has been teaching Aleena how to handle a crossbow and a firearm.

"We usually avoid using pistols or homemade bombs, but if it comes down to it, it's either us or them," Syra explained while showing how to position the crossbow. Syra mentioned, "While you might not see much action during your stay, the creatures don't appear all the time. However, when they do show up, we're usually ready for them, which is why we have watchers in place."

"Watchers?" Aleena asked.

"Yes, the men stationed in the towers, are always on alert," Syra replied.

"Do the goblin-like creatures ever attack?" Aleena pressed.

"Occasionally, but we usually manage to fend them off," Syra reassured her, noticing the unease in Aleena's eyes. "It's uncommon for them to venture this far. We're more likely to encounter them when we go out to gather wheat for bread."

She gave Aleena's shoulder a comforting pat and smiled. As Aleena absorbed Syra's words, she realized that her stay here was not meant to be permanent. Deep down, she longed to return home, missing her friends and family dearly. No matter how long it took, she was determined to find a way back.

After two weeks, Aleena started to acclimate to the rhythms of life in the community. She documents her time in a slightly weathered notebook she found, marking the weeks that have gone by. Enjoying leisurely walks, she relishes the opportunity to meet

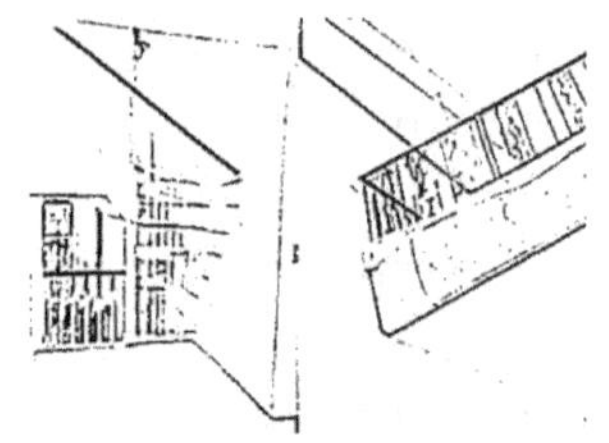

new people and engage in conversations. While she occasionally spends time with Eli, her main companion is Syra, and together they explore the abandoned houses that the community leaders have overlooked. In one particular house, Aleena noticed a balcony jutting out from the living room wall, yet it seemed completely inaccessible. There were no stairs leading up to it, and its position was alarmingly close to the ceiling. Adding to the house's strangeness, a set of stairs were warped in an odd manner, rendering them nearly impossible to navigate without a serious effort to climb. The overall atmosphere of the house left Aleena feeling both confused and a bit on edge.

"That's so strange," she thought, as she gazed at the interior. It has been two days since Aleena's exploration alongside Syra. They explored abandoned houses and buildings for anomalies that need to be recorded and labeled dangerous, unlivable. As Aleena adjusts to the community, she learned that many years ago, the first settlers of this forsaken town recognized the power of community and banded together to create a small but thriving colony. This revelation struck Aleena profoundly, as it highlighted humanity's remarkable ability to adapt to even the most unusual circumstances. She was assigned a room in a charming, vintage three-story building that exuded the character of the 1930s. The architecture, with its intricate details and nostalgic charm, made her feel as though she had stepped back in time, adding to the sense of wonder and possibility

that surrounded her in this unique place. She is living alone in a cozy studio apartment and is doing her best to adapt to the circumstances. Adjacent to the building where Aleena resides, there is another building that is used as a hospital. It has four floors and enough rooms to meet the community's needs, although not many require it unless they sustain serious injuries during their scouting missions or while patrolling the outer rim. The community is supported by three doctors and a handful of nurses but some of the women are currently undergoing training to provide assistance at the hospital if needed but considering that almond water provides magical properties, it’s rare that anyone gets sick. The bathrooms are quite small in the building where Aleena lives, but they come with a sink and toilet with no water running through the pipes, as expected. The tub is made of enamel-coated cast iron and somewhat clean. The room that Aleena is staying in is somewhat tidy, which made Aleena feel a bit more comfortable, but she still chooses not to sit in the tub, instead she takes a sponge bath by standing in the tub, then she pours a gallon of filtered almond water over herself while lathering up with a bar of soap. It’s the best that she can do. In the community, residents rely on almond water collected in large metal buckets during the rain showers. This valuable resource is primarily used for bathing and personal care, with each person receiving a set number of gallons to ensure everyone has enough for

their daily needs. Careful management of this water reflects the community's commitment to sustainability and resourcefulness, making each drop count in their daily routines. Almond drinking water is distributed in six packs, poured into empty glass milk bottles. Each person can only possess three packs per week depending on the amount of rain gathered in large amounts. This process not only ensures that everyone has access to almond water but also fosters a sense of community. Aleena has often pondered why almond water is the primary beverage in the Backrooms, but that remains an enigma that might never be solved. It's been almost a month since Aleena and Eli arrived, and both are doing well. Eli Marsh resides in the same building as Aleena, though his room is on the third floor. There seems to be quite a few people living in that building too. Eli seems to be integrating well into the community and has no plans to return to his former life. Although he has yet to talk about it with Aleena, he will do so in time. That day, the community threw a small party at the town hall, to welcome newcomers and to celebrate life. There was a lot of food and music. The tunes came from speakers connected to an old turntable that seemed to be from the 1950s. Aleena thought it was really cool that someone had managed to locate a turntable, speakers, and records. They probably found them in one of the houses and brought them to the community town hall. In a previous conversation, Syra explained to Aleena that when the town showed up in the Backrooms, it just came as is. She mentioned that items tend to pop up out of thin air in the Backrooms and when they appear they intend to

use them. Aleena noticed that all the buildings and houses in the town appeared to be stuck in the 1950s, however some buildings look older. She found it intriguing and promised herself to dig deeper into its history later. She frequently pondered whether the town's first inhabitants were transported along with the town.

"The Backrooms," Aleena murmured softly. "I thought it was merely an online story or a creepypasta," she clarified to Eli, taking a sip of punch that had a subtle almond flavor. He shrugged, not paying attention. They observed as the people reveled in the festivities. The punch was almond water with mixed Kool-Aid packets; Aleena made a sour face as she swallowed it. As people chatted and swayed to the music, Aleena stood out in her stunning outfit. She donned a yellow floral hippie-style blouse, elegantly tucked into a long denim skirt. Her black velvet Mary Jane shoes fit comfortably on her feet. The outfit she put together didn’t exactly scream 1950s nostalgia, but it was a spontaneous choice made from whatever she could find at the local thrift store just the day before. As she rummaged through a box of lost and found items, she encountered a colorful mix of garments from various decades. She couldn’t help but wonder who the clothes belonged to. She asked Syra about the clothes and Syra mentioned that when scouts go out to search for food and other necessities, some of them bring back clothes that they find in various crates and cardboard boxes. Eli's outfit made him appear quite dashing. He donned a short-sleeved, pastel blue button-up shirt paired with slacks and black shoes.

His hair was neatly styled, though he still had some stubble on his face. Eli looked over at Aleena. "Wow, you look beautiful," he praised, admiring her appearance. She blushed and looked away. A faint smile appeared on her lips. "I found the clothes in a huge lost and found box at that thrift store down the street."

"Me too, I also found my clothes there. They obviously have no clue who the original owners are, but it's great that they can provide newcomers with the necessities they need." Once again, Eli's gaze roamed over her appearance, making her feel a bit awkward.

"I was curious if you'd be interested in a dance," he asked. Aleena was surprised but figured that a single dance won't do any harm. They swayed to an old tune called, *A Summer Place*. A young man, appearing almost the same age as Aleena, glanced at her shyly. However, she was oblivious to his gaze, and Eli was eager for another dance with her. As he mingled with the crowd, he found his way to Aleena. Hesitating slightly, he introduced himself, "Hi, I'm Brian." Dressed in an olive-green button-up shirt and black slacks, he exuded a certain charm, enhanced by his bushy brows and striking blueish-green eyes. "Oh, hello, I'm Aleena," she responded warmly, shaking his hand. Meanwhile, Eli, who had been deep in conversation with another man, caught sight of their interaction. A pang of jealousy surged within him, prompting him to excuse himself and

approached them. "Hi, I'm Eli Marsh," he said as he introduced himself to the young man. Brian extended his hand for a shake. "I apologize, Sir, but I was hoping to speak with your daughter, if that's alright." Eli felt a twinge of offense, and Aleena caught the look in his eyes as they conversed.

"Actually, Eli isn't my father; we just happened to end up together." After reflecting on her words, she realized that her statement didn't quite convey what she intended. Her cheeks turned red.

"Yep, I get it. The first time I wandered into the Backrooms, I felt completely lost, scared and alone. Fortunately, I came across a middle-aged man named Chris, who was also trying to find his way out of the yellow maze," he pointed at the man with slightly curly salt-and pepper hair, medium built and has a five o'clock shadow. She noticed a gold wedding band on his left ring finger. His eyes are a shade of grey-blue, and he is somewhat taller than Eli.

"His story is incredible; you really should have a conversation with him," Brian suggested.

"What year was it before you ended up in this twisted dimension?" Aleena asked.

"I believe it was 1980. I was 18 and on my way to my friend's house on my bike. There was a short tunnel that I had to go through before getting to his neighborhood," he paused. "The tunnel became dark, and it wasn't dusk yet. When I went through, I ended up peddling straight into a wall. When I looked around, I found myself in the Backrooms." Aleena thought about what he said for a moment. "We ended up going through a yellow door and ended up in the yellow maze," Eli said.

"Well, we're still in the process of getting to know the people here, and I'm eager to learn more about the history of this town, I'll go to the library tomorrow," Aleena remarked.

"Great, the library holds everything you need. Each of us has contributed to the town's history by documenting our personal stories," Brian shared.

"Aleena and I will join you tomorrow," Eli added. Aleena looked puzzled, her brow furrowing as she wondered why Eli appeared to be dismissing Brian.

"Meet me at the library tomorrow after lunch. I think you know where it's at." Aleena nodded and smiled. Brian and Aleena enjoyed a dance or two while Eli mingled with the men and women at the gathering. Everyone in the town is at least over 18 years old. There are no kids present. Brian was just 18 when he first entered the Backrooms, and he looks the same as he did back then. However, he has since aged significantly. Time moves differently in the Backrooms. While there are few young adults in their 20s, most of the people Aleena encounters are over 30. The oldest resident is a man in his 50s, who knows more about the town's history than most people. Aleena remains unaware of Eli's age, but it doesn't really matter; they both found themselves in the Backrooms and journeyed together as fate intended. One of the men presented two bottles of wine, mentioning that he had obtained them from the wine cellar in one of the restaurants in the town. "Let's get the party started!" He exclaimed and gestured another man to help him with a medium wooden crate filled with several wine bottles. The man who brought the wine bottles, is in his 30s,

sporting a ruggedly handsome face, short black hair, and captivating hazel eyes. While looking around the room, Aleena sees that most of the guests are paired up, with just a few, including Aleena and Eli, still single.

"Each month, we honor Life and the fact that we've made it through another day in the Backrooms is amazing," Syra remarked as she walked over to Eli and Aleena. “Numerous individuals have decided to stay and carry on with their lives in this location, yet just a few chose to leave,” she paused and added, “They vanished without a trace, never to be seen or heard from again.” Aleena took a moment before asking, “Did they leave alone or in a group?"

Syra looked at her and replied, "A few went alone, but the other three set off together. There were two men and a young woman, about your age. Kyle and I were wondering if they ever made it to another colony."

"Are there other colonies in the Backrooms as well?" Aleena asked.

"Yes, there are. Kyle and I came from one of those other colonies. We were part of the raiders, which is how we know a lot about them and their methods. As you know, this town wasn't always here; it actually materialized out of nowhere in the wheat fields."

"What can you tell us about this town?" Eli asked.

“Well, there is more info about it at the library if you wish to read more. There is at least one original inhabitant of the town, but he doesn’t attend the parties, he’s kind of a recluse.” Aleena looked at Eli. “It looks like Kyle is looking for me, I’ll see you guys later,” she winked at them as she turned and

walked away. “I am curious about this town, I wonder how it suddenly appeared and what happened to the original inhabitants,” Aleena said as she took a sip from the glass of wine that Eli and she picked up from a table where other glasses were set. A woman in her late 30s, sporting long blonde hair and brown eyes, who was a bit on the heavier side, was arranging the wine glasses on the table. Aleena realized that the wine had a really rich flavor to it, especially since the label indicated it was from around 1910. As the party started to wind down, Aleena and Eli exchanged their goodnights with other people and made their way back to the building where their rooms are. Eli grabbed two bottles of wine to take with him.

"What do you think? Should we enjoy a little nightcap?" he proposed with a mischievous smile.

Aleena yawned, "I’m not sure, I feel like I’ve had my fill." She chuckled.

"Oh, come on, just for a little while," Eli urged playfully.

Aleena sighed, "Alright, but only for a brief moment."

They headed to the building. As Aleena stepped into his room, he secured the door behind him.

11

Aleena's First Time

"I can't believe that the case of bottles Josef brought were nearly gone," Aleena said with a laugh. "This is some great stuff," Eli added, taking a sip from the bottle. Aleena agreed, recalling the time she had wine at her cousin's wedding with her friends. They all got drunk, and the next morning, Aleena woke up nursing a hangover. "Um, Eli, if we found a way to go back to our world, would you be interested in doing so?" Eli pondered her question for a moment before responding bluntly, "No."

"But why not?"

"There are a few things I've done that I really regret, and I don't want to go back to that," he mentioned, gulping hard as he took another drink of the wine. He doesn't want to take responsibility for his past actions and the poor choices he has made in his life. The expression on his face showed his remorse. Aleena furrowed her brow and nodded in agreement.

"It appears that the others are unaware of who Eli is, so it's understandable that he wishes to remain here, especially with all his troubles back home waiting for him," she mused. A moment of silence passed between them, and then she continued, "I get it," glancing at him, she added, "But I want to return

home. I can't establish my home here. I want to be with my friends, my family, and my cat," a soft smile grazed her face as pleasant memories surfaced of her loved ones. Eli nodded and took another sip from the bottle. He handed the bottle to her, and she took another sip. They sat on the only couch in his room, chatting.

"How old are you, really?" Aleena asked. Eli hesitated before responding.

"I'm 35," he watched her reaction, concerned that she might reconsider spending time with him due to his age. "And what about you?" Eli swiftly redirected the focus away from himself.

"I told you already," she responded.

"Oh, yeah," he said.

"Well," she paused and continued, "I'm 21, but my birthday is in two weeks, so I'll be turning 22. However, I don't know how old I really am now. Time here feels different compared to where we came from. I can't help but wonder if my birthday has already passed." Her brow furrowed in thought as she pondered this idea. She fears that her family is frantically searching for her.

"I started marking down in a composition notebook the number of weeks we've been here."

"Why bother," he said.

"It matters to me," she responded as she took another sip from the bottle. They continued their conversation for a bit longer, as they both finished a bottle, and started another one. A wave of lethargy washed over them. Eli noticed the wine stain on Aleena's skirt before she did, but it hardly mattered as she leaned her head against his shoulder, seeking comfort.

He smiled warmly as he carefully lifted her and placed her on the bed, then reached for his cotton pajama shorts to put on her after removing her skirt. As he removed her skirt, a surge of desire coursed through him, and he began to caress her legs, marveling at the softness of her skin. "It must be the almond water. It makes the skin soft and beautiful," he murmured. Aleena, feeling lethargic, slightly opened her eyes to catch a glimpse of his face above her, a tender expression etched in his face. As his lips brushed against hers and his hands explored her body, she barely noticed the weight of him pressing down. Initially, she held back, unsure of his intentions, but soon his allure proved irresistible, and she surrendered to the moment. In no time, they found themselves intertwined in a passionate embrace. After their intimate encounter, they lay in each other's arms. Eli covered Aleena with a warm blanket. He got out of bed, stood up and let out a yawn. Stretching, his naked body barely visible in the dim light of the room, he turned and glanced back at her. She had fallen asleep, and he decided to dress her in his pajama bottoms, leaving on her beautiful yellow blouse. Their beautiful intimate encounter was very delightful, and he could tell she never had been with anyone before. He was her first.

"You look so beautiful," he thought to himself, while observing her as she slept. He slipped into a pair of soft plaid style pajama pants paired with a simple

white tee shirt. With a sense of ease, he made his way to the couch and settled in, pulling a cozy blanket over himself. This particular level of the Backrooms seems to be caught in a perpetual midday, a strange phenomenon that somehow aligned with the body's innate need for rest. In this peculiar town, everyone adhered to a shared rhythm, which explains why most residents are currently lost in slumber while the guards dutifully rotated their shifts, keeping watch over the stillness that enveloped them.

A gentle kiss, tender and sweet, can weave a thread of connection, a moment where hearts align, whispering secrets only they can understand. Yet, beneath the surface of that fleeting touch lies a deeper truth: the bond forged between two souls is unbreakable. In the quiet corners of their hearts, they carry the imprint of each other.

12

Another Day in Paradise

As Aleena opened her eyes, the unmistakable sensation of a hangover hit her.

"No," she murmured. The urge to vomit was overwhelming, and she couldn't hold it back as she stumbled into the tiny bathroom. After retching into a metal bucket placed beside the toilet, which was devoid of water, she grabbed a white cup from the sink, filled it with almond water, and swished it around in her mouth. She exhaled deeply and gazed at her reflection. Her eyes appeared tired; almost blood shot; she still had on the yellow blouse, but she realized she was not in her skirt—rather, she was dressed in a pair of cotton blue men's pajama shorts. She hurried out to find Eli asleep on the couch. She regarded him with suspicion, her heart raced. Suddenly, she felt the urge to vomit again and hurried back to the bathroom. Her eyes landed on the bottle of almond water.

"This will help me feel better," she thought, gulping it down, she started to feel better. "It's amazing that this strange water has magical properties," she said to herself. After taking care of business in another bucket, she returned to the bed but noticed her skirt lying on the floor. She frowned and struggled to recall what had transpired a few hours ago.

Reclining on the bed, she exhaled deeply. Eli was snoring away. She rolled her eyes and turned onto her side. A few minutes later he started to wake up, yawning as he slowly sat up, rubbing the sleep from his eyes. He spotted Aleena on his bed, watching him with a suspicious gaze; her arms crossed.

"What's the matter?" he asked.

She shook her head and let out a huff, saying, "What's the matter?" She frowned. "Well, let's see, why am I in your pajama shorts?"

"Oh that," he sighed and said, "You spilled wine on your skirt and um," he paused, choosing his words carefully, "you changed into the shorts, but I guess you don't remember." Aleena cannot remember but it will come back to her eventually and she may not be happy about what she remembers. She felt an odd ache between her legs, so she got out of bed and went into the bathroom. It was then that she noticed some blood on her panties.

"Maybe I started my period,' she thought. She walked out of the bathroom, still looking at Eli with suspicion.

"Thank you for the shorts," she said with a soft smile. She picked up her skirt. "Damn it, I liked this skirt, it fits really well."

"And it looks beautiful on you," Eli remarked awkwardly, trying to ease the tension in the room.

"I should go back to my room and change. Will you be going to the library today?" she asked him.

He shook his head, "No I'm good." He gave her a smile. "Maybe we can have lunch together?" he suggested. Aleena smiled and nodded. However, a sense of suspicion still lingered in the back of her

mind. Something happened, something she can't remember. Her hair was a bit disheveled, and as soon as she returned to her room, she took the time to comb it out. She noticed that she wasn't bleeding anymore and shrugged it off as one of those odd moments. Later, she made her way to the library. The library was always open, and books were scattered all around. She was on the lookout for anything that might provide her with additional information about the town. She stumbled upon several books, primarily school yearbooks and a town almanac.

"A town almanac," she whispered to herself. She discovered another book and brushed off the dust. It contained details about the town and its history, with the town's name displayed on the cover.

"Ashley," Aleena murmured to herself. She noted that the town's population was listed as 679, which struck her as strange since it felt like there were fewer people living there now. She settled into a chair, surrounded by a few books resting on the table beside her. The details she found were quite elementary, and none of the books provided her with a definitive understanding of what had transpired in the town or why it had ended up in the Backrooms. She let out a sigh and recalled what Syra had mentioned about a man who could be one of the original inhabitants. *"I recall Syra saying he's a hermit; perhaps Eli and I could pay him a visit,"* she pondered. Brian entered the room, saying, "Hey, you're here." His smile widened as Aleena glanced up at him. He took a seat beside her. She expressed her curiosity about how the town came to be in the Backrooms and mentioned that she was

searching for details about its residents. "I honestly have no knowledge about this town, except that when Chris and I were discovered by Kyle and Collin, they brought us here."
"What is Syra's and Kyle's back story?"
Brian hesitated then said, "I heard that they were exiled from the community they belonged to, because they were caught stealing but It's just a rumor," he shrugged.
"Oh, I see," Aleena responded but chose not to press for further information about them.
"I was wondering if you could perhaps show me where the recluse lives."
Just then, Eli entered the room. "Hey, there you are! I thought we were supposed to grab lunch together." His eyes landed on Brian, and Brian could sense the tension.
Brian said, "I can take you to Harold right now if you want, but just a heads up, he might not answer. Usually, folks just leave a note under his door and drop off supplies at the front." Aleena furrowed her brow, "Front door? Does he live in a house?"
Eli is seated beside Aleena, now focused on their conversation. "Yes, it seems he has his own house. Syra thinks he is one of the town's original inhabitants. Likely the only one left. The rest of us came after the town appeared in the Backrooms."
"Okay, take us," Aleena said. The three of them exited the library and strolled a few blocks away. Brian appeared somewhat nervous since nobody

really engages with Harold, and those who do, only speak to him from behind his front door. As they reached the door, Aleena knocked softly. A voice from within responded, "I'm fine, don't need anything right now." She exchanged glances with Eli and Brian before clearing her throat. "Um, Mr. Harold, my name is Aleena, and my friends and I would like to speak with you, if that's alright." There was no reply, prompting Aleena to try once more.

"Harold, I was hoping to get some details about the town's history and any memories you might have." He didn't respond, but just as Aleena, Eli, and Brian were about to head out, the door creaked open. A man in his fifties appeared, sporting scruffy salt-and-pepper hair and wearing a dirty beige coat with faded jeans. His hazel eyes narrowed as he regarded them with suspicion. He seemed a bit fragile and slightly emaciated. She looked at him earnestly, expressing her desire to understand the town's history and what had transpired. "Were you here when it happened?" she asked, her voice trailing off. Brian leaned closer and whispered, "Of course he was here." Eli fixed his gaze on Harold, contemplating the weight of the man's experiences, realizing that he had undoubtedly witnessed something truly horrific. Harold narrowed his eyes, clearly wary. He asked, "What's got you so curious?" She hesitated for a moment before responding, "Eli and I just arrived here, and I heard

you were around when the town...well, when it became part of the Backrooms." Harold exhaled deeply and nodded, acknowledging Aleena's curiosity.

He warned her, "I know you might think I'm a bit out there, but here it goes." Aleena pressed him for his story, and he continued. "I had just returned home from work, and my wife and son were at her sister's house for a birthday party."

He excused himself and took a bottle of almond water from his big ice box before returning to his seat.

"I was by myself when I first heard the screams outside. I stepped out to see what was happening and spotted Mrs. Jenkins staring up at the sky. When I looked up too, there was," he paused, a distant expression crossing his face. "A bizarre black void loomed in the sky, casting a shadow over the entire town. One of my neighbors dashed back inside, likely to alert the authorities in the nearby town of Haze. Suddenly, the ground began to tremble, and as the darkness expanded, chaos erupted among the townsfolk. I felt the panic rise within me as I attempted to call my wife, but the line was dead. Things took a strange turn when people began claiming to see their deceased loved ones." Harold recounted a particularly unsettling incident where a woman cried out, convinced that her son had come back, even though he had passed away years earlier. Aleena listened intently, captivated by his tale. Eli urged him to keep going, clearly intrigued by the bizarre occurrences that Harold experienced. Harold inhaled deeply, feeling the weight of the moment. "People began to vanish without a trace, prompting

me to rush inside and secure my door. Peering through the slats of the blinds, I saw the town swallowed by an ominous darkness. An eerie silence enveloped everything, and then, without warning, a powerful earthquake struck. The house trembled violently, making me feel as if it might collapse right from under me. In that terrifying instant, I screamed and prayed for safety. It all happened so quickly." Harold finished off the last of the almond water, while Eli, Aleena, and Brian contemplated the situation. Brian broke the silence, asking, "what happened next."

Harold shrugged and replied, "I finally found the courage to leave my house, realizing that I was alone and with no one around, I decided to stay in my house no matter what. Only venturing out if necessary. Eventually people began to show up." Eli's skepticism lingered as he asked, "How did you manage to survive? Where did you find food and water?"

Harold replied, "I had stocked up on water and canned goods, particularly spam, for emergencies, but that supply only lasted about a month and a half. I soon realized it rains frequently in this area, so I began collecting rainwater. However, when I took a sip, it tasted like..." He hesitated, knowing Eli would understand what he meant to say.

"Almond water," Brian finished his sentence. Aleena nodded in agreement. Eli believes that as more people arrive in town, Harold tends to withdraw. Although the locals were familiar with him, they often regarded him as an eccentric. Aleena looked over at Eli and Brian before saying, "Thanks, Harold, for sharing

your story." After they left, Aleena and Brian headed to the diner located down the street to eat. Meanwhile, Eli opted to return to his apartment but made a brief stop at the restaurant where the man from the party picked up the wine bottles. As he entered, he noticed a couple of people sitting in booths, each absorbed in their own activities. In the back of the establishment, the cook was busy at work while a waitress stood by, waiting to see if Eli was interested in a meal. In the colony, the concept of money was foreign; everyone contributed to the community without expectation of payment. Unlike his previous life, where mortgages and financial transactions were the norm, the Backrooms operates on a different principle entirely. Eli caught the waitress's eye as she made her way toward him. He couldn't help but be drawn to her gentle smile, captivating hazel eyes, and full lips, finding her undeniably attractive. Loneliness had been his constant companion, and he yearned for the warmth of affection, hoping that Aleena might be the one to fill that void. He doesn't want to push her away, so he chooses to take it slow. He was cautious, not wanting to pressure her into a relationship that could make her feel uneasy. She seems to be unaware that they had sex the previous day. Perhaps she forgot but she obviously had more on her mind to think about what had happened the other day. The waitress, with a playful wink, broke his reverie, asking, "So

sexy, what do you want to eat?" Her light brown hair is neatly tied back in a ponytail, with soft bangs brushing against her forehead and she appears to be a few years older than Aleena. She is dressed in a blue and white waitress outfit; she caught Eli's attention. A smirk grazed his lips as his eyes scanned her appearance. He asked, “What’s your name?”

“Molly, and yours?" He introduced himself as Eli Marsh and then hesitated before asking what her plans were for later. She raised an eyebrow, clearly impressed by his directness. Eli let out a nervous laugh and replied, “I was just curious and…” She cut him off with a playful tone, suggesting, “No worries, we can hang out if you want.” He responded with a knowing smile and a nod, feeling a sense of ease between them.

Eli said, “I’ll just have toast and ham.” The waitress chuckled, “There’s no ham here, but I could get you toast and spam.”

Surprised, Eli asked, “how did you get spam?” The waitress took a seat beside him and explained that scouts explore the vast grocery level, bringing back whatever they find. It turns out they’ve stumbled upon cans of spam in the aisles, which have become their primary source of meat. Eli grimaced at the thought of Spam, viewing it as food for the less fortunate. Spam is something he would never eat and despite its popularity, he had never actually tried it.

“That's intriguing! Where did the wine bottles come from?”

“Most of them were sourced from this restaurant and another one further down the street,” she said adding, “We intended to save them for special occasions, like

that party we hosted." Eli felt a twinge of guilt for having taken two bottles without permission. With a slight smile, he suggested, "Perhaps we could enjoy a bottle together later." She laughed and nodded, saying she would check with the cook before heading off to give the cook Eli's order. After he finished his meal, he told the waitress where he's staying and left to look for Aleena, assuming that Brian and she were at the Diner, but they weren't there. He assumes that they had gone to the library after they ate.

13

Finding Out New Information

Aleena looked at Brian with curiosity. "I have a question," she said, pausing for a moment. "When the scouts head out to gather food and supplies, how do they know which door will lead them back here?" Brian took a sip of his almond water and remarked, “I’ve only visited the endless grocery level once or twice. There is a door that leads directly to that level and back, but scouts must time their visits carefully, as access to that level is restricted to specific times of the day.” Aleena looked confused and asked how anyone could tell the time in a place that seemed perpetually stuck at noon. Brian nodded and explained, “We gauge time by how people feel; when folks start to feel tired, it is a sign that it is nighttime even though outside it’s never nighttime. It’s really that simple.”

Aleena chuckled, “Okay, I guess.” She accepted the explanation. After a brief pause, Aleena asked, “When is the grocery level accessible? When can people visit that level.” Brian contemplated for a moment before responding, “it’s usually available around seven in the evening.” With that information, Aleena nodded, and they exited the library, parting ways as they headed off in different directions.

After a long day of training alongside Syra and another woman, Aleena headed to her small apartment. As she approached, she glanced up and noticed Eli's light glowing in his room. A thick fog was rolling in, and fatigue washed over her. She pondered whether it was already 10 PM back home as she ascended the stairs to her apartment. Pausing briefly, she decided to pay Eli a visit. Upon reaching his door, she was taken aback by the unmistakable sounds of intimate moans emanating from within. It was clear that Eli had company, and a frown crossed her face as she processed it.

She sighed, clearly unimpressed, and muttered to herself, "Well, I guess he doesn't need company." With a roll of her eyes, she turned away and headed to her room, where she promptly locked the door behind her. She lay awake in the dim light, her thoughts swirling like autumn leaves caught in a brisk wind. The door that could take her home lingered in her mind, but before she could grasp that comforting thought, a sudden memory jolted her. It was of the day before, a passionate encounter with Eli that unraveled unexpectedly. As the memory flooded back, she bolted upright, shock etched across her face. "Oh no," she whispered to herself, the weight of realization anchoring her to the moment. Laying back down slowly, she found herself staring blankly at the ceiling, the intimacy of their connection now tangled with uncertainty. As she recalls his caresses and kisses, there is an ache, a deep desire to be with him. Then a tinge of jealousy shadowed her heart. As she lay in her bed, the turmoil of her emotions swirled relentlessly within her. With a sigh, weariness

overcame her, and the turmoil subsided into a bittersweet, dreamless sleep. Hours later, she stirred from her slumber, stretching her limbs and yawning. She couldn't help but wonder what the day had in store for her. As she gazed out her window, the familiar midday light flooded in, a constant in her routine, with a soft sigh, she got ready. She slipped into a white tee, an olive-green vest, and her favorite jeans.

After dressing, she opened her door just in time to hear a woman descending the stairs. The woman in the waitress uniform waved goodbye, saying, "See you around, Eli." Aleena quickly shut her door but left it slightly ajar to catch a glimpse of her.

She couldn't help but scoff at the sight. She frowned and paused for a moment before stepping out of her room, locking the door behind her. Just then, Eli spotted her and rushed down the stairs.

"Hold on a second," he called out. She stopped and asked, "How did you sleep, Eli?" Her tone tinged with sarcasm.

"Pretty good, actually. I haven't slept like that in ages, well, not since I found myself in the Backrooms," he replied, with a faint smile appearing on his face. She shook her head and added, "I saw a woman leaving."

"I met her at the restaurant where she works, and I ended up inviting her over to my place." Aleena laughed softly, saying, "Eli, you really don't need to share your personal life with me. If, spending time

with her makes you happy, then I'm happy for you." He glanced at her, taking in her appearance, but she quickly averted her gaze. He suspects that she remembers what went on between them. She shyly glanced at him and averted her gaze once again when she noticed he was staring at her. Aleena shared that she would be part of the lookout group today.

Eli asked, "Syra asked you to join the group?" She confirmed with a nod.

"Brian's not going with you?" Aleena glanced at him, and she clarified that Brian had other plans. Eli felt a wave of relief knowing that Brian wouldn't be around, but he can't shake the feeling that he's being a bit selfish by wanting all her attention. The truth is, he struggles to connect with the other townsfolk since most of them hail from different eras. Even Molly, whose company he genuinely enjoys, is from 1996. Aleena, on the other hand, knows about him, and there's a certain comfort in that familiarity that he craves, additionally she is from his timeline. He finds her very attractive. Despite her awareness of his wrongdoings, he is still drawn to her intelligence and allure. Aleena interrupted his thoughts, "I'll be patrolling the inner ring fortress of the town to ensure its security."

He nodded in agreement, saying, "Okay, I'll join you, it gives us some time to explore the rest of the town." Aleena chimed in, "Yeah there's something I want to check out." Eli raised an eyebrow, intrigued by her remark. "What is it?" She then revealed her discovery about a door that might lead back to their world. "You still want to go back?" he questioned. Her desire to return was evident in her eyes.

He paused, and she hesitated before turning to face him. They stood in the middle of the street, tension hanging in the air. Eli expressed his concern, “I don’t think you should attempt it.” Aleena sighed and stated firmly, “I understand that you don’t want to return but I do.” With determination, she headed toward the Diner, where Syra and the rest of the group are gathering. Eli watched her walk away; arms crossed in disbelief. After a moment of hesitation, he shook his head and decided to follow her.

14

A Terrible Incident

Aleena and Eli set out to explore the town's streets, focusing on the houses believed to be vacant. As they walked past Harold's place, they sensed he might be watching them from behind the curtains, but it didn't faze them. Their mission was clear: to investigate the empty homes for any signs of unusual activity. Eli glanced at Aleena as he secured his pistol back into its holster.

"Did Syra mention what we should be on the lookout for?" he asked. They walked closely together, but Aleena's mind was elsewhere, distracted by thoughts that had little to do with their mission. Eli halted her momentarily, recalling Syra's instructions.

"Oh, right. She said we need to check for any abnormalities in the residences."

“What does she mean by abnormalities?” Eli asked.

“Houses that have unusual structures within,” came the reply. Eli's confusion deepened. He pressed, “What do you mean?”

“If a house appears distorted in any way inside, we are instructed to mark the door, and someone will arrive to seal it off to prevent entry,” Aleena paused before adding,” Syra, informed everyone but I guess you weren’t listening, because you were too busy

flirting with Molly." She rolled her eyes and smirked at him. He scoffed in response,

"Oh, now I see, you're jealous." Aleena arched an eyebrow and shot him a disapproving glance, shaking her head in frustration.

"Hold on a sec, no I'm not jealous," she lied.

"If you say so," Eli teased.

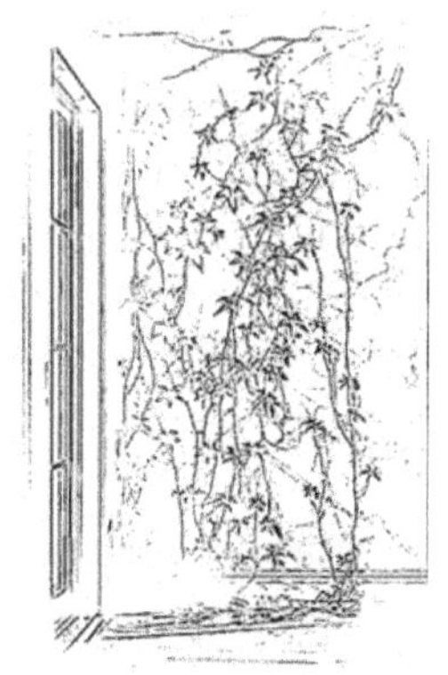

Aleena frowned and said,

"We need to check out that house, so, let's focus on our task," she insisted. Together, they approached a dilapidated white house, where several boards on the fence lay broken and scattered. The door creaked slightly ajar, and Aleena felt an unsettling vibe about it. They exchanged a nervous glance and took a deep breath before entering.

As soon as they stepped inside, they noticed dark vines creeping along one wall of the Livingroom. Suddenly, something caught Aleena's attention, and she gasped as a shadow darted into another room. She gestured to Eli, and they both drew their weapons. Aleena glanced around and saw the walls of the old house subtly shifting. The wallpaper began to resemble the patterns from the yellow maze, making her uneasy. She urged, "We should leave, now." Eli shot a quick glance at her; he moved toward the room where the entity had vanished. Just then, Aleena clutched his arm, her eyes wide with concern as she slowly shook her head. She leaned in and whispered, "Do you want to end up back in the yellow maze?" The possibility of ending up back in the yellow maze

is strong. The urgency in her gaze made him pause, realizing that this was more than just fear; it was a serious warning. He gave her a quick nod, and they hurried out of the house. However, as soon as they stepped outside, the entity lunged at them, knocking them to the ground before it sped away down the road.

Aleena exclaimed in dismay, “No,” and without hesitation, she and Eli raced back toward the town hall building. As they entered, they saw Syra with a raised rifle, aiming at them but once she saw who they were, she lowered the rifle.

“What happened?” she asked, then suddenly they heard screams and dashed out. A man was being torn apart by a *Hound*, a terrifying creature that lurks in nearly every level of the Backrooms. His screams echoed as the creature viciously clawed at his leg, leaving a scene of horror in its wake. Syra, Eli, and Aleena fired their weapons at the creature, but it was Kyle's shotgun blast that finally brought it down.

Two other men quickly followed up by throwing a net over the beast, ensnaring it. They will manage to take it outside the colony. One gives the final blow that will end its life. Aleena looked around, uncertainty in her eyes, and asked, “What do we do now?”

With a heavy sigh, Syra replied, “We need to burn the body when he dies.”

“Why?” Eli asked.

“He will turn into one of them and that’s a fate worse than death,” she responded. Two individuals transported the injured man to the hospital. With just two doctors currently present and a handful of nurses

on duty, Aleena felt uncertain about his chances of survival. Later, she and Eli found themselves at the Diner, where the mood was heavy. Aside from the cook and two waitresses, only four other people occupied the space, contributing to the overall somber atmosphere. Aleena was filled with sorrow over the man who ultimately succumbed to his injuries, and his body was incinerated. Nevertheless, she shared with Syra the story of the house from which the Hound had emerged. Soon after, the structure had been boarded up with old wooden planks, its windows obscured and the door firmly sealed shut. The men carefully secured a bright yellow tape around the perimeter of the structure, marking it off with precision and intent. Eli, sensing the weight of the moment, leaned closer to her, his expression softening as he reached out to take her hand in his.

"Don't feel bad about what happened," he reassured her, his voice steady and comforting. The warmth of his grip offered a small solace amidst the chaos that happened a few hours ago. Aleena sighed, her voice trailing off as she began, "I understand, but…"

Eli quickly cut in, his tone firm yet understanding. "But nothing," he replied, taking a moment to gather his thoughts.

"It wasn't your fault; it was something we couldn't have predicted, and it's truly unfortunate." Aleena nodded in agreement, her expression softening as she processed his words. Just then, the waitress approached their table, placing their meals in front of them with a warm smile. "Thanks," Eli said appreciatively, and they both dug into their food. After finishing their meal, they made their way back

to the building where they were staying, the soft rain was cool and yet refreshing. Eli had a bottle of wine ready for them in his room, a small gesture to help ease the tension after the day's surprising twists. Aleena, however, couldn't shake off the weight of what had happened; the memories would linger with her, casting a shadow that she would carry for the rest of her life. Eli invited her to his room, suggesting they could have a more in-depth conversation there. Aleena responded with a gentle smile, her eyes reflecting a mix of curiosity and apprehension. "Okay," she agreed, and as they settled in his room, the atmosphere shifted. As their discussion unfolded, Aleena's emotions began to surface, and tears streamed down her cheeks. She confided in Eli about her fears, expressing a deep-seated anxiety that she might never return home. In a comforting gesture, he wrapped his arms around her, offering solace in her moment of vulnerability. But then, as if drawn by an unspoken connection, he leaned in and pressed his lips softly against hers. To his surprise, Aleena didn't pull away.

A fleeting moment can shift the course of fate,
A tender kiss ignites a tempest of feelings,
Yet can such warmth withstand the shadows of the Backrooms, where nightmares linger and hope is all but lost?

15

Curious Vanishings & Other Revelations

Aleena is keeping a detailed journal of her experiences in the colony, meticulously noting the passage of days and weeks as she settles into this new environment. As she writes, she can't help but observe a peculiar phenomenon: some of the homes around the town seem to be vanishing without a trace. At first, she thought it was just her imagination playing tricks on her, but as time goes by, she becomes increasingly aware of the empty spaces where houses once stood. The quiet disappearance of these homes adds an unsettling layer to her daily routine. While she shares her thoughts and observations with others, she keeps this particular concern to herself, feeling a mix of curiosity and unease about what might be happening to the colony, in general. The house that the Hound bolted from weeks ago, has vanished without a trace. Strangely, no one seems to recall it ever being there, yet they all remember the man who was attacked by the Hound. She asked Molly if she recalled the events, and Molly replied that the Hound somehow breached the fortress around their town and attacked Will. Aleena looked at her, puzzled, but chose not to argue, as her memories differed from others. So, she decided

not to mention what she had been witnessing, even Eli doesn't know. Their relationship has been marked by his relentless pursuit since their first intimate encounter. Aleena often tries to distance herself from him, yet there are times when she finds it impossible to do so. He sometimes waits outside her door, and while she occasionally lets him in, she makes a deliberate effort to keep their discussions from becoming too personal. Still, there are moments when intimacy feels inevitable. Although she could refuse him, an unspoken obligation complicates her choices. It's difficult for her to understand this feeling, especially since their only connection stems from the Backrooms; before that, they were strangers who likely would never have met. This unsettling reality lingers in her mind, especially when she recalls their first intimate moment together, which was not only her first sexual experience but also left her with a lingering anxiety about the possibility of pregnancy. Since stepping into the Backrooms, she has noticed something unsettling: her menstrual cycle has completely vanished. This absence raises a troubling question in her mind, *could she possibly be dead*? However, she quickly shakes off that dark thought, realizing it's not a conclusion she can accept. Instead, she resolves to bring up her missing periods with Syra, hoping that she might have some insight or explanation for this bizarre phenomenon.

In her mind, she sees herself as a 21-year-old woman, however, the peculiar nature of time in the Backrooms leads her to suspect that she has aged. Even though her reflection remains unchanged, she feels the same. It's a strange dissonance; an unsettling awareness lingers in her mind, hinting at the passage of time that seems to operate differently in this strange dimension. She suspects that others have also stopped aging. After having lunch with Brian, Aleena stopped by the Diner to see Syra. She found her mingling with other local women, as two tables had been pushed together to accommodate everyone. The table was adorned with plates of food and glasses filled with rich red wine, creating a lively atmosphere. The women were laughing and chatting, clearly having a great time, and Aleena was no exception, she was enjoying herself too. Molly was part of the group, but Aleena felt a bit uneasy around her. It wasn't that she held any grudges about Eli; rather, it was the fact that Molly was unaware of the intimate history between Aleena and Eli that made things feel awkward. She suspects that Molly, who is a few years her senior, might actually have feelings for Eli, but she could be mistaken in that judgment. As for her own emotions towards Eli, she's uncertain. She's hesitant to get too close to anyone since she plans to leave eventually, and the thought of saying goodbye to friends is something she finds hard to bear.

As the party ended, Aleena learned that the women in town gather once a month to discuss issues that affect them. While not every woman participates, a significant number do show up for these meetings. The town has a population of about 150 residents, which is notable but still far fewer than the number of people who once lived in *Ashley* before the town was split and one half sent to the Backrooms. After the women departed, leaving only Molly and Syra, Aleena seized the moment to ask about the missing menstrual cycles.

They lounged together, savoring the last bottle of wine, the dim light casting a warm glow around them. Aleena took a deep breath, her mind racing as she contemplated how to broach a sensitive topic.

"Syra, I've been meaning to ask you something," she began, her voice tinged with hesitation. "Ever since I ended up in the Backrooms, I've noticed that my period has completely stopped. Do you have any idea why that might be happening?"

Syra, seemingly unfazed, shrugged her shoulders and let out a dismissive scoff, as if the question was trivial in the grand scheme of their bizarre reality. "I'm not entirely sure, but I've heard other women here are going through the same thing."

Molly chimed in, "it's probably a good thing, especially since getting pregnant in this place is the last thing anyone wants." Syra opened up about her situation, revealing, "My periods have also ceased, but at my age, it hardly makes a difference." Aleena, intrigued by this revelation, asked, "Do you have children?" With a heavy heart, Syra responded, "Yes, I have children back home, but they were already in

their twenties when I went missing." As she spoke, a wave of sorrow washed over her, and her expression shifted, reflecting the painful memories of her family that she left behind.

Molly said, "My periods have stopped too, and the concept of aging is a thing of the past here. I'm 30 years old, but I appear somewhat younger than my actual age because this weird dimension seems to cancel aging." Aleena looked at her perplexed. "How old were you when you came to the Backrooms?" she asked.

"I was 23," Molly responded.

"Oh, wow, time is different here," Aleena said. Molly continued talking. Aleena listened intently, as she processed Molly's words, perhaps reflecting on her own perceptions of age, the changes that come with it and how she too will not age at all, so long as she is in the Backrooms.

"Maybe Molly's not so bad," Aleena thought, as a soft smile grazed her lips. Later, Aleena excused herself and made her way back to her room, her expression a mix of contemplation and sadness. As she climbed the stairs, thoughts of her family filled her mind, wondering if they were searching for her. She pictured them putting up flyers with her face on them, declaring her missing. With a heavy sigh, she reached her door and opened it. As she pondered on her return home, a swirl of questions filled her mind. Would she step through the door only to find that time had slipped away from her, leaving her to confront a version of herself that felt foreign and aged? How long has she truly been in the Backrooms? The uncertainty gnawed at her, making

her wonder if the price of her journey would be a dramatic transformation, a stark reminder of the time that had passed. Would she return to a world that had moved on without her, or would she find that she had changed in ways she couldn't yet comprehend? She entered her room and shut the door behind her, assuming Eli was preoccupied with another woman since Molly was out with Syra. Honestly, all she wanted was to unwind, be alone for a while. She quickly changed out of her clothes and put on a nightgown she had found in the lost and found box. It was made of delicate lace and smooth satin, featuring a soft pastel mauve hue reminiscent of styles from the 1950s and early 60s. After brushing her hair and washing her face, she collapsed onto the bed, letting her eyes flutter shut. A haunting silence surrounded the building, with the streets outside devoid of any sound, no birds, no sounds of cars, etcetera, it seemed eerie to her. Soon, she would venture to the seemingly endless grocery level, hoping to discover a door that might lead her back home.

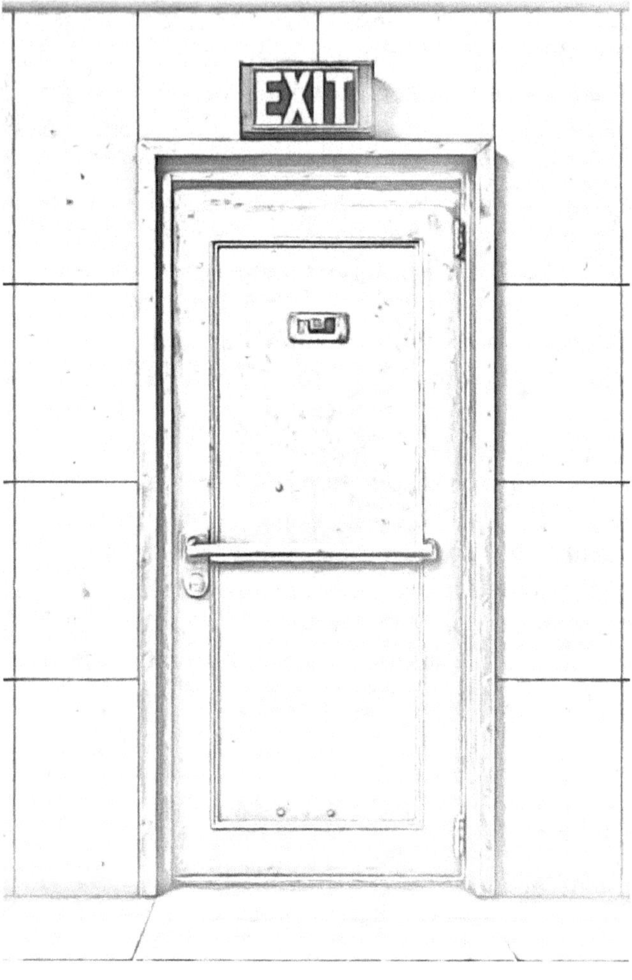

16

The Door

It has been six months since Aleena and Eli first set foot in the colony, and gradually, the number of vacant homes is dwindling, leaving behind a sense of unease. One evening as Aleena and Eli were chatting in her apartment, she finally discussed with Eli what she had been noticing in the past couple of months. They settled on the couch, her fingers nervously tracing the fabric as she gathered her thoughts. With a deep sigh, she breaks the silence that envelops them.

"Eli," she starts, her tone calm but laced with an undercurrent of worry, "think back for a moment. Do you recall that day when the man was attacked by the Hound?" He nodded. She then asked, "Where were we when that happened?" The question hangs in the air, a reminder of the chaos that has begun to intertwine with their everyday existence, and she watches Eli's expression shift as he processes the memory.

"We were at the diner," Eli started but his words faded as he struggled to recall the details. Aleena let out a sigh and shook her head, then shared her own memories of the event, leaving him stunned by what she revealed.

Initially, he found it hard to accept, but the earnestness in her gaze urged him to dig deeper into his own recollections. Slowly, fragments of the past began to resurface. Suddenly, he exclaimed, “Oh shit, I remember,” though confusion still knitted his brow. He looked into her beautiful hazel eyes and asked, "What’s going on?"

She replied, "Something's happening in the town, and I’m worried we might vanish too.” Eli nodded thoughtfully, adding, "Everyone seems to be here for now, but since Harold rarely goes out, we can't really know if he's still around." Aleena exhaled deeply, her mind swirling with a mix of emotions and reflection. She understands that her perspective might not sit well with Eli, yet she feels compelled to voice her concerns.

“Despite the comforting sense of safety that this place offers, this is not a permanent solution. The reality is that no matter how secure we feel, the day would inevitably come when we must leave,” she paused letting out a soft sigh. “When we join the scout team in a few days, we should check out the layout of that level. Even though it may seem endless, I’m sure there’s a door somewhere.” Eli let out a deep sigh, his head nodding in reluctant understanding. "Alright, when we get there, we can explore a bit, but we shouldn’t leave just yet," he stated. Before he could finish, Aleena cut in, her voice tinged with

frustration, "But why not?" The exasperation in her gaze was unmistakable, revealing her eagerness to journey back home. He didn't give her an answer. Later, after visiting Brian at the library, Aleena decided to stop by Harold's place, but to her surprise, all that remained was an empty lot where his house once stood. She wanted to talk to Harold about the strange happenings but now he is gone. Approaching the site, she felt a strange tingling sensation in the air, almost like static electricity, heightening her sense of unease. Backing away slowly, she abruptly turned and hurried toward the building where she is staying. She dashed up the stairs and knocked on Eli's door. Laughter echoed from inside, and she muttered to herself, "Damnit, he's with someone right now." She exhaled deeply, her thoughts pressing down on her as she retreated to her room. Gazing out of the grimy window, she found herself lost in contemplation, trying to make sense of the bizarre occurrences unfolding around her.
"Where did the houses disappear to?" she thought. The view beyond the fortress wall that surrounds the small, ever vanishing town, was still discernible. However, as she looked over at some of the structures down the street, she saw the subtle changes in the landscape, a reminder that time was slipping away and each tick of the clock seemed to echo in her mind,

amplifying her sense of urgency and confusion as she tried to piece together what was happening around her. As Aleena stood in her apartment, she was jolted by the piercing sound of a woman's scream echoing through the stairwell. Her heart raced, and she instinctively furrowed her brow in concern. Without a moment's hesitation, she swung open her door to investigate the commotion. To her surprise, she spotted Mary, a fellow resident of the building, hurrying down the stairs with a look of panic etched across her face. It was clear that Mary had just emerged from her own room, and the urgency in her movements suggested that something was seriously amiss. Aleena's mind raced with questions as she watched Mary's frantic descent, wondering what could have caused such a distressing outburst. Aleena hurried down the stairs after Mary. Eli heard the commotion and followed Aleena downstairs. Emerging from Eli's room, a woman with short brown hair styled in a pixie haircut and rosy flushed cheeks, caught Aleena's attention as she glanced up. The woman was wearing a rose mauve slip dress that clung to her figure, and her short brown hair was slightly tousled. She did not follow them down. "Eli, what's going on?" The woman called out, her voice laced with worry as she glanced down, watching Aleena and Eli running down the stairs. Meanwhile, Aleena managed to reach Mary first. "What happened?" Aleena asked. Mary inhaled deeply, her voice trembling as she recounted

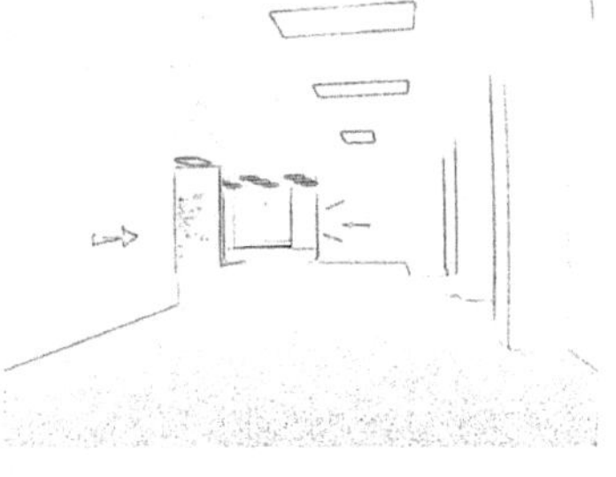

the unsettling experience to Aleena. “I was in the bathroom, just finishing up my routine, when I glanced at my reflection in the mirror,” she began, her words laced with a mix of disbelief and fear. “That’s when I saw it, the yellow maze. It appeared right in the mirror, vivid and intricate. I glanced behind me and for a second or two,” she paused. “It looked like I was back there again.” As she spoke, tears began to flow down her cheeks, which had grown slightly hollow from the weight of her emotions. The sight of the maze had shaken her to the core, leaving her feeling vulnerable and exposed, as if the very fabric of her reality had been altered in that fleeting moment. Aleena furrowed her brow in confusion and asked, “What do you mean?”

Just then, Eli made his way toward them in the lobby, his expression a mix of curiosity and concern. Mary, feeling the weight of the moment, reiterated her unsettling experience. The air thickened with tension as Aleena and Eli exchanged a worried glance, both sensing the gravity of the situation. “I’m not going back in that room,” Mary declared, her distress evident in her voice, as she stood firm in her decision, clearly shaken by whatever had transpired within those four walls. It seems that everyone has found their way into the Backrooms via the *non-Euclidean* yellow maze, and it's easy to see why Mary is feeling so distressed. Her experience was harrowing; she barely managed to escape the

labyrinthine corridors, that seem to stretch endlessly. Aleena and Eli exchanged a knowing glance as they settled onto a wooden bench by the lobby window. With a tone of genuine concern, Aleena reassured Mary by saying, "I believe you." Her recent observations about what's been happening in the town made Aleena anxious. Meanwhile, Eli, oblivious to his attire in just his boxers, prompted a sigh and an eye roll from Aleena, who couldn't help but grimace at the situation. The woman who was in his room earlier was dressed and heading downstairs. She paused to ask, "What's going on?"

Aleena recognized her as the manager of the local shop where residents pick up their daily essentials. She is the person responsible for collecting signatures in a notebook, ensuring that individuals receive the items they need, although groceries must be sourced from a different store. Eli recounted what had happened, and her reaction was one of genuine astonishment.

"Oh no," she exclaimed, her eyes widening in disbelief. "Eli, I think I'll have to avoid coming back here, this is truly disturbing." Her concern was palpable, reflecting a deep-seated fear of the unknown consequences that could arise from returning to a place where strange happenings had taken place. Aleena scrutinized the woman more closely, noting the way her almond-shaped blue eyes sparkled with genuine concern. The delicate crow's feet at the corners of her eyes hinted at Claire being in her mid-thirties. She's dressed in a lovely sundress over her slip dress that features a delicate mauve lace design, with thin spaghetti straps that gracefully highlight her

shoulders. The dress falls mid-calf, and on her feet, she sports a pair of brown clogs that have a retro vibe, reminiscent of the 1970s. She must've picked out the clothes and shoes from the lost and found box. "Don't worry, Mary, we're here for you, and nothing will happen to you," she reassured her gently. Aleena shifted her gaze from Eli to Claire, sensing the tension in the air. Eli swallowed hard, fully aware of the unspoken thoughts racing through Aleena's mind. Meanwhile, Mary rubbed her eyes, a gesture that revealed her distress, and nodded in agreement, murmuring, "I know, but what I saw was terrifying." Claire, sensing Mary's fear, placed a comforting hand on her shoulder, offering silent support in this moment of vulnerability. The air was thick with concern, as each of them grappled with the weight of the situation. Claire turned to Eli with a warm smile and said, "It was nice sugar, but I'd prefer we just stay friends." Eli felt a slight flush creep up his cheeks as he nodded in response, his expression surprisingly calm. It was clear he wasn't disheartened by her decision to keep things platonic, and there was a hint of understanding in his eyes. Meanwhile, Aleena, who had been observing the exchange, couldn't help but smirk at Eli's reaction, as if she found the whole situation amusing. After Claire left, Aleena realized it was only a matter of time before the entire town learned about what had happened. A few hours later, Eli and Aleena joined the group of people that were going to the endless grocery store level. As Aleena stepped through the door, she couldn't help but wonder if it might lead her back home. *"Maybe if I came alone,"* she mused.

Eli caught her gaze, sensing her thoughts. He suggested they gather what they needed and head back to town. She nodded in agreement, but deep down, she was already plotting her escape. Around them, people strolled by with woven baskets brimming with groceries and other essentials. After they finished gathering the items, they headed toward the door.

"Let's move quickly; the door will only be visible for a few more minutes," Syra urged. Aleena and Eli were the last to step through, and as Aleena turned to look back, she saw the door vanish.

"Until the next time," Aleena softly murmured. They exited the house that led to the grocery level and took the baskets to the town hall where things will be sorted later. The group of people that ventured out of town to gather wheat arrived an hour later. The wheat is made into bread. Aleena was tired and after the events of the day, she headed to her building. As she walked down the street, Eli approached her and walked into the building with her. Aleena paused as she glanced around. "Eli, I think we should consider moving to another building."

"Why?" he asked, as they made their way up the stairs.

"What would happen if this building disappeared while we were in it?" she asked with a hint of worry. He sighed, understanding what she was implying. "I'm sorry if I keep holding you back from leaving but I think it's dangerous for you to do it alone," he said. She chuckled, "Ever the knight in shining armor, aren't you," she responded playfully. They entered her apartment.

He did not leave but he decided to stay with her for the night—well, whatever is considered nighttime in this level of the Backrooms. Aleena is consumed by a growing anxiety as homes and buildings vanish into thin air, and she can't shake the feeling that the house with the door leading to the grocery level might be next. As Eli sleeps peacefully beside her, completely unaware of her turmoil, she feels a pull toward that mysterious door, a gateway to the unknown that beckons her with the promise to lead her home.

17

Goodbye

It has been three weeks since Aleena last ventured into the infinite expanse of the grocery level. While she hasn't gone to that level lately, she has noticed several more buildings have vanished, and a few homes have also disappeared, including one that was still occupied. The unsettling changes prompted the locals to organize a town hall meeting that very day, drawing a large crowd of concerned residents eager to discuss the implications of these losses. The atmosphere was charged with anxiety and curiosity as neighbors exchanged worried glances, each person grappling with the uncertainty of what these developments might mean for their community and its future. Syra stepped up to the podium, her presence commanding the attention of the gathered crowd. With a warm yet serious tone, she began, "Hello neighbors, I realize that our town meetings are typically planned well in advance but today is different. There are pressing matters at hand that require our immediate attention and discussion." Her words hung in the air, signaling the importance of the moment and the urgency of the issues that needed to be addressed. The audience shifted in their seats, curiosity piqued, as they prepared to hear what was unfolding in their community. Syra mentioned that Aleena had observed some homes and buildings

mysteriously disappearing. When called upon to share her observations, Aleena recounted her experiences, detailing the unsettling moments when she noticed structures that had simply vanished from sight. After she spoke, she returned to her seat beside Brian and Mary, while Eli sat next to Rick and Molly, one row behind her. Mary then approached the podium to share her story. Once everyone had finished speaking, Syra once again addressed the audience.

"It's hard to say what's really happening, but if you notice anything unusual, don't hesitate to speak up. If some of you feel the need to leave because you're worried about disappearing, that's your call. Just remember, if you choose to venture beyond the wheat fields, you'll encounter challenges and hidden dangers at every turn." Some people nodded in agreement while others remained silent. Aleena had made her decision; the next time she visited the endless grocery store, she would find a way to slip away. In the meantime, she plans to move out of her current building into a one-story house that appeared ready for occupancy. Aleena noticed no strange occurrences inside it, at least none that she was aware of. With only a few belongings to gather, she quickly packed what she could into her backpack and placed it beside the sofa. As she settled onto the sofa, lost in thought, a knock at the door interrupted her contemplation, Eli stopped by. "Aleena, it's me," he said. She recognized his voice and sighed, knowing he was likely there to convince her to stay. They weren't married, and she had no plans on it either. Their bond that connects them is limited to the Backrooms. She recognizes him for who he truly is, a

stark contrast to the rest of the town, who remain unaware of his real identity. After a second knock, Aleena stood up and opened the door.

"Eli, what brings you here?" she asked as she let out a frustrated sigh.

"Are you planning to move out?" He leaned against the door frame.

"Yeah, I'll be staying with Mary. She said she doesn't trust living in this building anymore." Eli's expression was filled with concern as he entered the room. Aleena let out a sigh and welcomed him in, and they settled onto the couch together.

"I understand, but I really wish you would think it over," Eli said, gently resting his hand on her knee. In response, she placed her hand over his, offering a soft smile, her warm and compassionate gaze meeting his. He leaned in for a kiss, but she instinctively pulled away after their lips met. She reassured him and said, "I'll just be down the street. I won't be far." He nodded, a grin appearing on his face. Later, Aleena moved into the house where she and Mary would be roommates. While she anticipated Eli would come by for visits, she had no idea he was considering moving in as well. Aleena was careful not to reveal the intimate relationship she had with Eli, uncertain of how Mary would react to the news. She felt a twinge of concern as she subtly tried to dissuade Mary from accepting Eli's offer to move in with them. When Mary pressed her for reasons, asking why she thought it might not be a good idea, Aleena let out a resigned sigh. She replied, "I just thought you'd prefer to live with other women." This comment was meant to steer the conversation away from the complexities of her

own situation while also planting a seed of doubt in Mary's mind about the arrangement. Mary glanced at Aleena with curiosity before saying, "Aleena, I'm into men." It dawned on Aleena that her earlier remark had been misinterpreted. "Oh, I didn't mean it like that," she quickly clarified. "I'm not gay."
Mary chuckled and replied, "No worries, I kind of assumed you weren't, but honestly, I'd be flattered if you were." They both burst into laughter. Mary joked about her looks, saying, "I might not be the prettiest girl around, but I wouldn't turn down anyone who found me attractive, regardless of whether they were a man or a woman." Their laughter continued as Aleena began unpacking her things in her new room. The room felt smaller, a stark contrast to her spacious bedroom back home in the other world, which now seemed like a fading memory. The one-story house features three bedrooms, a single bathroom, a kitchen, and a modest living room. It wasn't anything fancy or elaborate; it embodied the typical charm of a 1950s home, one of the few still standing strong, with electricity still flowing through its wires. It always piqued Aleena's curiosity. She often found herself wondering how some structures in town managed to have power. It's just another mystery that will likely remain unsolved. She quietly gathered a few essentials, including the knife she discovered, which now hangs from the sheath on her belt alongside a

gun holster for added flair. Her plan is to explore the house with the door that leads to the grocery level. However, since she's going solo, there's a chance the door could lead her somewhere unexpected, and she's actually hoping for that twist. While Aleena, Mary, and Eli enjoyed a light dinner in their new home, their conversation meandered through various topics. Aleena, then asked, "I hope you don't mind me asking, but what other levels of the Backrooms have you encountered?" After a brief pause, Mary took a sip of her almond water, nodding thoughtfully. "Before I arrived here, I found myself in a hotel that seemed to stretch infinitely upward, with floors that never seemed to end." She hesitated, gathering her thoughts before continuing. "It was a bizarre and disorienting experience. I had no weapons, and when a death moth began to pursue me, I fled in sheer panic. I stumbled into an empty room and quickly locked the door behind me, my heart racing as I sat on the bed, fixated on the door, bracing for the moment it might burst open. When the relentless banging finally ceased, I cautiously rose to inspect my surroundings, checking every nook and cranny for hidden threats. The thought of opening the closet door filled me with dread, as I imagined a creature lurking within, ready to drag me into the abyss. To ensure my defenses, I wedged a chair under the closet doorknob, ensuring that nothing could jump out. To my astonishment, I discovered that this level had electricity; a working phone sat on the nightstand, a rare glimmer of normalcy in an otherwise chaotic environment. I attempted to reach out to my husband, my heart racing with the hope that he would pick up the phone.

Instead, I was met with a disheartening click, followed by silence." Mary let out a weary sigh as she recounted her experience, revealing that she had spent several days confined to that room.

"I finally summoned the courage to open the door and peer cautiously into the deserted hallways. With each step, I moved deliberately, avoiding the windows and remaining vigilant for any lurking entities that might be watching me."

Aleena, intrigued by Mary's story, asked, "What type of creatures did you encounter in that ominous level?" Eli, sitting nearby, felt a twinge of unease at her curiosity, suddenly realizing that her interest might stem from a desire to leave the comforts of the town. Mary told them about what type of creatures she encountered. Eli shifted uncomfortably in his chair, the weight of the moment pressing down on him.

"As I stepped through the door, I found myself in the grocery level, where a group of people had discovered me and brought me here." A distant look shadowed her face as she reflected, "It feels like ages ago." She took a sip of her drink, while Eli and Aleena exchanged glances. Aleena considered the unpredictable nature of the doors, realizing the importance of staying alert as she navigated through the various levels. Later, after their meal, Aleena joined Mary in the kitchen, marveling at the town's enduring electricity, a sentiment that Mary readily echoed. Despite the eternal afternoon outside, and the endless fog, they instinctively knew when it was time to rest, so they settled in for the night. Eli was on duty as a watchguard, unaware that Aleena had quietly slipped away, leaving a brief note for Mary and a

more detailed one for him. Her heart raced as she approached the house with the door, a mix of fear and excitement coursing through her. With a backpack filled with essentials, a weapon holster, and determination, she pressed on. Meanwhile, Eli, stationed in one of the lookout towers, felt a sense of unease wash over him.

He scanned the area meticulously, but everything seemed normal. Relaxing, he thought of Aleena, a soft smile creeping onto his face as he reassured himself, convinced she wouldn't actually leave.

"She won't leave," he said to himself. Hours later, a new guard arrived to take over the watch. He headed to the house where he was staying, only to find that Mary was absent and Aleena was nowhere in sight. As he searched the room, he examined her belongings, and just as he was about to leave, something caught his eye, a letter resting on top of the drawer. Eli picked it up, opened it, and began to read the message addressed to him. He whispered a quiet "no" the weight of the moment pressing down on him. In a rush, he made his way to Mary's room, where he found a similar envelope resting on her pillow. He hesitated, knowing instinctively that it contained a farewell message. A wave of heat rushed to his cheeks as he turned away, retreating to the living room where he hastily grabbed a backpack and a few weapons he could manage to carry. Without a second thought, he bolted out of the house and sprinted down the street, his heart racing.

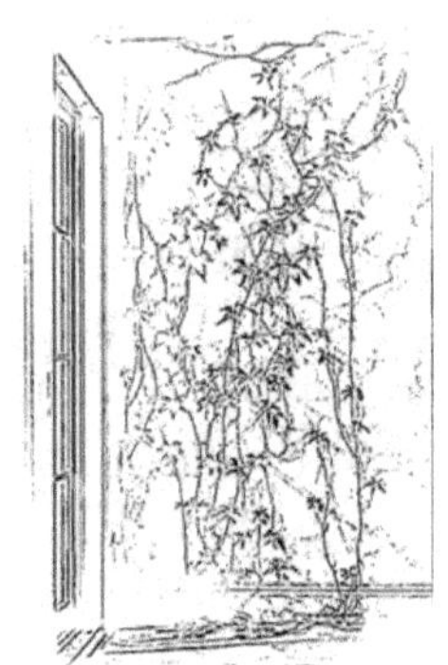

He paused at the Diner, where the familiar scent of coffee and breakfast filled the air. Molly looked up from behind the counter, her expression curious. “Eli, what brings you here?” she asked, wiping her hands on her apron. “Did you see Aleena?” he pressed, urgency lacing his voice. Molly nodded, her brow furrowing slightly. “She stopped by about an hour ago, ordered scrambled eggs with toast. She seemed a bit down, though. When I asked her what was wrong, she just shook her head and said it was nothing.” Eli felt a surge of anxiety wash over him. “Molly, I need to find her, and I might not come back,” he said, his voice thick with emotion. He leaned in and pressed a gentle kiss on her cheek, his heart heavy with regret. “Forgive me for being an ass,” he said, sincerely. Molly stood in the doorway; her brow furrowed in confusion as she watched him turn away, his silhouette gradually fading into the distance. He made his way back to the house where he’s staying and gathered necessities for the journey. He then went to the house that marked the entrance to the grocery level. With each step, a sense of finality washed over him; he understood that crossing the threshold meant there would be no turning back.

As he stepped into the shadowy interior of the house, his gaze was immediately captured by the eerie sight of dark vines slithering along one wall, their presence both strange and foreboding. These enigmatic tendrils seemed to emerge from nowhere, twisting and curling

in a way that suggested a life of their own. The dim light cast unsettling shadows, enhancing the feeling that something unnatural was at play, leaving him with an unsettling sense of curiosity mixed with apprehension about what lay ahead. Looking around, he noticed that the structure was beginning the stages of transformation into oblivion.

A chilling reminder of the house's impending fate. Despite the unease that settled in his stomach, he felt a surge of determination. “Aleena had been right all along,” he said to himself. With a deep breath, he steeled himself and pushed open the door, stepping into the unknown.

18

The Attic

Aleena found herself in a labyrinthine level constructed entirely of weathered wooden planks, reminiscent of a forgotten attic. As she treaded carefully through the sprawling maze, she observed that the space unfolded in a chaotic arrangement of oddly shaped rooms, each echoing with the creaks of the aged wood. The floor, walls, and ceiling were all fashioned from the same dark, timeworn timber, creating an oppressive atmosphere that seemed to close in around her with every step. There is no lighting, making the level quite dark. In the silence, the occasional creaking of massive wooden structures can be heard. As the unmistakable sound of creaking floorboards echoed through the dimly lit room, she instinctively froze, her heart racing in her chest. Gripping her knife tightly, she felt the cool metal against her palm. Although a pistol rested within easy reach, she was determined to reserve it for a moment of dire necessity, preferring the quiet precision of her blade for now. The shadows danced around her, and every creak seemed to amplify the silence, heightening her senses as she prepared for whatever might emerge from the darkness. As she pressed forward, a wave of uncertainty washed over her. "Where am I?" she pondered, her mind racing with

questions. Each step was deliberate, her feet carefully navigating the uneven terrain, wary of the creaking boards beneath her. The dimness enveloped her, the absence of light amplifying her unease, prompting her to pull out a flashlight. The beam cut through the darkness, revealing the worn edges of the floor and the shadows that danced around her. She felt a chill run down her spine, a mix of fear and curiosity propelling her deeper into the unknown. She reminisced about the warmth and safety of the town she left behind, a stark contrast to the uncertainty surrounding her now. A wave of regret washed over her as she thought, "I shouldn't have left." The rapid thumping of her heart echoed in her ears, a reminder of her anxiety, but just as she was about to take another step, an unsettling sound caught her attention. It was a chittering noise, reminiscent of teeth grinding, akin to the incessant gnawing of a rodent on something hard. The eerie sound sent a shiver down her spine, halting her in her tracks as she strained to identify its source, the shadows around her suddenly feeling much more menacing. The eerie sound echoed through the dimly lit attic, sending a chill racing down her spine. With a shaky breath, she gripped her knife tightly, as if it were her only lifeline in this moment of dread. The weight of the situation pressed heavily on her; she knew that her survival hinged on her next move. An unsettling presence inched closer with every heartbeat. She could almost sense the unseen entity lurking in the darkness, its intentions unknown but undoubtedly menacing. In that suffocating silence, she steeled herself, ready to confront whatever horror awaited her in the

depths of the decaying attic. She cast a quick look at her knife, a frown creasing her brow as she shook her head in disapproval. “This won’t do,” she murmured to herself. With a deliberate motion, she slid the knife back into its sheath, the familiar click of metal against leather echoing in the tense silence. Her heart raced as she reached for her pistol, the cold steel feeling both reassuring and intimidating in her grip.

Taking a deep breath to steady herself, she aimed the weapon at the approaching figure, her throat tightening as she prepared for whatever was about to unfold. Suddenly a piercing screech sent a jolt of adrenaline through her veins, causing her heart to race as it broke the silence. Her eyes widened in disbelief as she beheld the horrifying sight approaching her, a monstrous rat, an astonishing five-foot-long creature barreling toward her with alarming speed. Panic surged within her, but she quickly regained her composure, instinctively reaching for her weapon. With a steady hand, she fired several shots, the sound of gunfire echoing in the still air, until finally, the creature collapsed, its massive body thudding against the floorboards.

As the creature took its final breaths, she decided to put it out of its misery, plunging her knife into its side multiple times to hasten its end. With a sense of grim determination, she rummaged through her backpack and pulled out a flashlight, its beam cutting through the dimness to illuminate the scene. The light fell upon the enormous rodent revealing its grotesque features and matted fur. She couldn't help but marvel at its size, a grotesque testament to nature's oddities, she examined the creature more closely, her heart

racing from the adrenaline of the moment. Its crimson eyes gazed vacantly into the void, devoid of any spark of life. The elongated, fang-like teeth, tinged with a sickly brownish-yellow hue, appeared menacingly sharp, suggesting they could slice through flesh with the same ease as a hot knife through butter.

"What do I expect in this godforsaken place," she said to herself. The contrast between the lifeless stare and the lethal weaponry of its mouth created a chilling aura, leaving an unsettling feeling in the air. Aleena let out a disconcerting sigh. Then she heard more coming, she ran. The endless attic went on forever. As she navigated the familiar surroundings, everything seemed to blend into a monotonous backdrop until she stepped into a hallway and was confronted by a massive moth. She halted in her tracks, bewildered. The absurdity of the situation struck her first, there were large rodents lurking behind her, and now this enormous insect was looming ahead.

She was resolute in her quest to navigate past the moth that obstructed the hallway. A feeling stirred within her that this path could lead her out of the bizarre, twisted attic. With a steady hand, she lifted her pistol and fired. The sound of the gunshot reverberated through the space, and the moth fell lifelessly to the ground. She dashed past it, the sound of large rodent feet scurrying behind her. As she sprinted down the endless corridor, she rounded a

corner and spotted a door. Taking a quick breath, she flung it open and slammed it shut behind her. The faint sound of scratching claws against the door echoed in her ears, a reminder of the creatures lurking just beyond the barrier. But then, as if a switch had been flipped, the noise abruptly ceased, plunging her into an unsettling silence. Curiosity piqued, she turned around, only to find herself enveloped by the shadows of a dense, dark forest. Towering trees loomed overhead, their gnarled branches intertwining like skeletal fingers reaching for the sky, while the ground was carpeted with a thick layer of damp leaves that muffled her footsteps. The scent of earth and moss, and an eerie stillness hung in the atmosphere. *"Now where am I,"* she pondered.

19

Faith & Hope

As Aleena ventures deeper into the foreboding forest, she becomes acutely aware of every sound and visual detail that surrounds her. The air is thick with an eerie stillness, punctuated only by the rustling of leaves and the distant call of unseen creatures. Shadows dance among the gnarled branches overhead, creating a patchwork of light and dark that plays tricks on her eyes. Each step she takes is accompanied by the crunch of twigs underfoot, a reminder of her solitude in this vast, untamed wilderness. She scans her environment, noting the twisted roots that snake across the ground and the faint scent of damp earth that lingers in the air, all while a sense of unease settles in the pit of her stomach. As she stood at a distance, her gaze was drawn to an unusual creature that emerged from the shimmering surface of the pond. Its form was undeniably otherworldly, evoking a sense of unease within her. The creature's skin, a delicate powder blue, was adorned with faint scales which seemed almost ethereal yet bizarre. With pointed ears that seemed to twitch at the slightest sound, it possessed a slender, elongated frame that defied any conventional notions of gender. She found herself pondering its nature, “Male or Female? Hell, I really don’t

know," she muttered. realizing that it bore no obvious signs of being male or female, leaving her to wonder about the mysteries of its existence. She quietly slipped behind a sturdy tree, her heart racing as she observed the creature ambling down the narrow path. Its movements were deliberate, each step echoing in the stillness of the forest, and she held her breath, hoping to remain unseen. Once it vanished from view, she cautiously emerged from her hiding spot, resuming her journey with a mix of relief and unease.

As she walked, her mind wandered to the weight of her pistol at her side, calculating the number of bullets left in the chamber. The thought lingered, a reminder of the potential dangers that lay ahead, and she couldn't shake the feeling that she might need every round. Finding a moment of relative safety, she settled onto a sturdy log and rummaged through her backpack.

Her fingers brushed against the bottle of almond water, which she eagerly pulled out, along with a sandwich she had prepared before leaving the colony. The familiar taste of the sandwich brought a sense of comfort as she took her first bite, savoring the flavors that reminded her of home. Just as she was beginning to relax, a distant sound pierced the air.

A siren wailing somewhere far off, its eerie tone sending a shiver down her spine and pulling her back to the reality of her surroundings. As she paused for a moment, she muttered to herself, "That sound is too far to identify." After finishing her meal, she gathered her belongings and continued on her journey. Following a narrow path, she soon emerged into a

clearing, where the grass danced in the gentle breeze. The trail stretched ahead, winding through the lush field and beckoning her to explore what lay beyond. On the far side of the field, a row of towering trees stood like sentinels. She felt a flicker of hope that perhaps beyond those trees lay a place that felt less intimidating and safe. Above her, the sky was draped in an unusual tapestry of lavender-hued clouds with gray, casting an ethereal glow over the landscape, while a light drizzle began to patter softly against her hair, adding a refreshing chill to the air. She touched her hair; moisture glazed her hand from the rain. She sniffs it.

"Yep, it is almond rain," she muttered. With a resigned sigh, she pressed on, her footsteps crunching softly on the damp earth, each step a mix of trepidation and anticipation as she ventured further into the unknown. She was halfway across the field when the siren blared again, this time much closer. Panic surged through her, and she froze, her heart pounding in her chest. Her hand instinctively moved to rest on the pistol at her side. Suddenly, from the trees at the edge of the field, a monstrous creature towering at 48 feet emerged, and her heart sank at the sight.

She gasped softly, "Oh no," she said. Her heart racing as she caught sight of the tall, gangly figure moving aimlessly nearby. The creature seemed oblivious to her presence, which gave her a fleeting sense of relief. With a quick glance over her shoulder, she turned and briskly made her way away from it, careful to keep her footsteps silent against the rocky ground. Finding refuge behind a massive boulder, she

crouched low, her breath shallow as she peered around the edge.

She focused intently on the creature, trying to decipher its next move while her mind raced with thoughts of escape. As the creature drew closer, its form became increasingly discernible, revealing a hauntingly gaunt physique. Its emaciated body was a disturbing sight, with ribs protruding sharply against its grotesque, reddish-brown skin, which seemed stretched taut over its skeletal frame.

The arms were unnaturally long and thin, resembling the limbs of a malnourished specter, with fingers that were bony and elongated, each tipped with long, jagged brown nails that looked as if they could easily tear through flesh. Its feet, equally elongated, bore three elongated toes that curled slightly, giving it an unsettling appearance as it moved with an eerie grace. The overall impression was one of a creature that had been starved not just for food, but perhaps of life itself, evoking a mix of fear and pity in her heart. Aleena's eyes grew wide as she absorbed the strange scene in front of her. Black wires twisted and coiled around the creature's torso, weaving in and out of its skin, and creeping upward toward where a head should have been.

As she finally glanced up, her jaw dropped in shock, and she instinctively covered her mouth to stifle a terrified squeal. The creature's head was a grotesque sight, featuring two sirens protruding from either side, but there was no actual head to speak of, just two siren horns.

The bizarre surreal combination of the wires and the sirens created an eerie, almost bio-mechanical appearance, like a giant cyborg, leaving Aleena horrified by the nightmarish figure before her. The creature's form resembled a bizarre assembly of mismatched parts, as if it had been cobbled together from a collection of discarded remnants. The most striking feature was the pair of sirens which appear to be its head but upon closer inspection, one could see that the insides of these horns housed gaping mouths, lined with razor-sharp teeth. This unsettling combination made Aleena unable to look away from the creature's haunting presence. The creature unleashed a deafening sound from its two mouths. It resembled the wail of an old 1940s city siren, mixed with a gurgling screech that sent shivers down Aleena's spine. Instinctively, she covered her ears to shield herself from the overwhelming noise. As the creature moved away, Aleena seized the opportunity to escape. She had no intention of returning to the forest; instead, she sprinted toward what appeared to be a trench ahead, in hopes of hiding from it. The creature locked its gaze on her, relentless in its pursuit, showing no signs of mercy. With each powerful stride, it closed the distance. For a moment, Aleena felt the chilling grip of fear as it nearly reached her. However, the refreshing almond water she had consumed coursed through her veins, igniting a surge of energy that made her feel vibrant and alive. With renewed determination, she pushed herself to run faster, her heart racing in rhythm with her pounding footsteps, as the sound of a siren echoed behind her, a constant reminder of the danger that

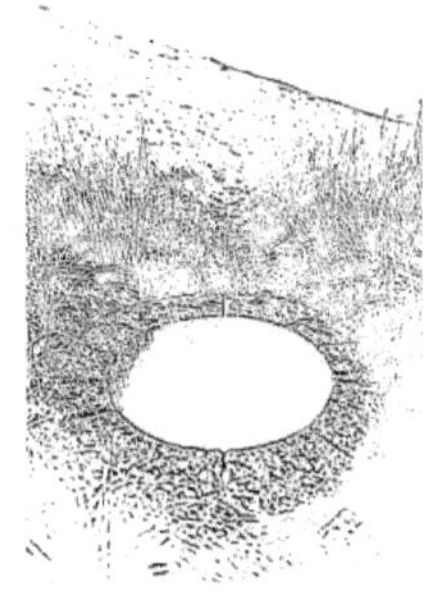

lurked just a breath away. Aleena sprinted toward the trench, where a murky stream snaked along the ground. Her heart raced as she spotted what looked like a sewer entrance. Glancing back, she saw the creature closing in on her, its menacing presence sending chills down her spine. Panic surged through her as she reached the entrance, diving inside just in time to escape its grasp. As the creature's menacing horn loomed closer, almost as if peering into the tunnel sewer, Aleena instinctively scrambled backwards. Her heart racing with fear. The moment it unleashed a piercing sound vibrating in the gutter hole, she became momentarily deaf and leaving her disoriented. In a panic, she pushed herself further away, her hands scrambling for purchase on the ground, but before she could regain her bearings, the ground beneath her gave way. With a sudden, terrifying drop, she plunged into an inky abyss, the darkness swallowing her whole as she fell, her mind racing with thoughts of what lay below. As she plummeted through the sewer, a sudden beam of light illuminated her descent, and before she knew it, she found herself spiraling down a vibrant pool slide. Splashing into the cool, water below, the impact sent ripples across the surface. She instinctively kicked her legs to resurface and her heart racing with adrenaline. Once she broke the surface, she quickly unstrapped her backpack, feeling the weight of it tugging at her as she swam towards the edge of the pool. With determination she dragged the bag along the tiled

edge, finally tossing it over to safety. She hoisted herself over the edge and with a soft thud, she settled onto her back next to her backpack. She gazed up at the stark white tiles of the ceiling above. The mysterious, unexplainable light source doesn't have a clear origin, making the lighting seem to come from nowhere. She closed her eyes and exhaled, gradually rolling onto her side. Her eyes scanning the room as she took in her surroundings.

Meanwhile, Eli navigated through seemingly endless corridors that had a distinctly futuristic vibe. The sleek design of the area not only highlighted advanced technology but also created an overwhelming sense of isolation. He clung to the hope that Aleena might be at this level, but deep down, he knew that was a long shot. As he pressed forward in his search for an escape, a sense of discouragement began to wash over him. Each step he took seemed to amplify his isolation, making the vastness of his surroundings feel even more daunting. It was as if the path ahead was designed to lead him deeper into solitude, and with every moment, the weight of loneliness settled heavier on his shoulders. He swallowed hard, realizing he was utterly alone in this desolate place. The only sound that broke the silence was a mechanical hum that seemed to echo in the distance. Each time he moved closer to the source, the noise would recede, almost as if it were teasing him. Stopping in his tracks, he took a moment to reflect on the situation. It felt like a deliberate distraction, pulling him away from whatever he was searching for, leaving him to question whether he should pursue the sound or trust

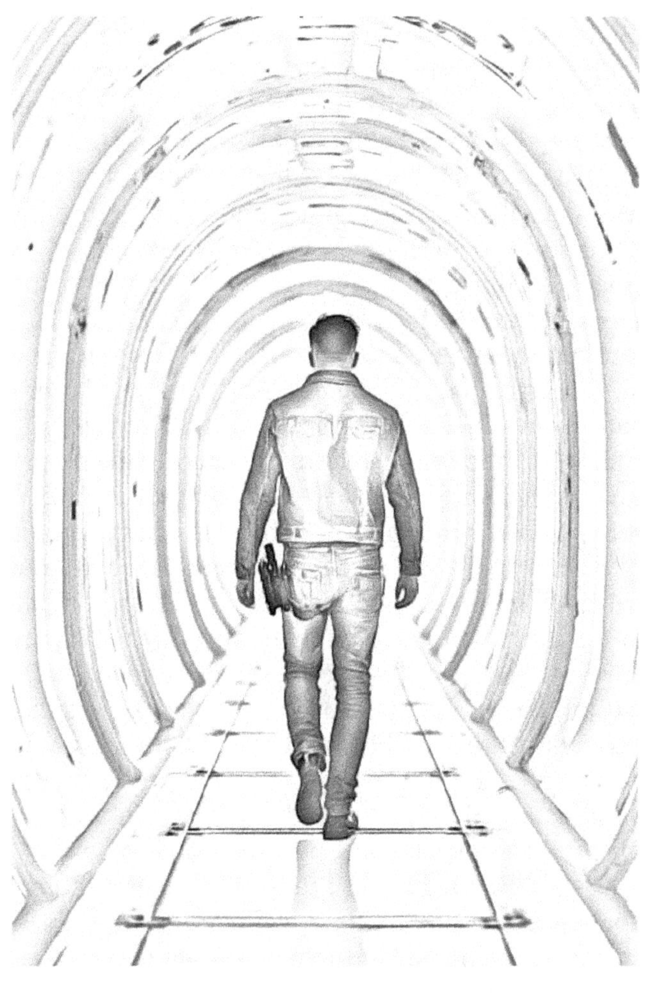

his instincts to stay put. “I think I’ll head the opposite direction,” he said to himself. As he wandered through the brightly lit corridor, a door suddenly slid open with a soft whoosh, revealing an inky blackness that seemed to swallow the light around it. He hesitated at the threshold, his heart racing as uncertainty washed over him. Should he venture into the unknown, or was it wiser to turn back? The silence was thick, almost palpable, and curiosity tugged at him. With a resigned sigh and a hint of defiance, he muttered to himself, “Well, what the hell,” and stepped into the darkness, ready to embrace whatever lay ahead. He suddenly found himself standing at the foot of a staircase, each step gleaming with pristine white tiles that seemed to reflect the light in a soft, inviting glow. The walls surrounding him were also clad in the same immaculate white tile, creating a seamless and almost surreal environment that felt both sterile and oddly comforting. The only contrast to this sea of white was the sleek metal handrail, the cool surface offering a stark yet elegant touch against the bright backdrop. The tiles gave the space an almost clinical feel, drawing him further into the unknown. He spun around, his heart sinking as he realized the door had vanished without a trace. A heavy sigh escaped his lips, a mix of frustration and disbelief, as he took in his surroundings. With a sense of resignation, he began to make his way down the staircase, which twisted and turned into a dizzying spiral. The air was thick with unshakeable tension, and he couldn't help but wonder what lay at the bottom of this winding staircase.

20

Reunited Again

Aleena wandered through the poolrooms, her curiosity piqued by the unusual atmosphere surrounding her. “This place is strange,” she murmured under her breath, taking in the surreal beauty of the shimmering water that reflected the soft light above. Despite the soothing aroma of almond water wafting from the pools, which momentarily eased her tension, she felt an undeniable urge to keep moving. She reminded herself, *“I have to move on.”* Although she hadn’t encountered any creatures yet, she remained on high alert, her senses heightened as she navigated the enigmatic poolrooms. As she explored the area, she decided to take a quick dip in one of the pools. The water was crystal clear and inviting. Its soothing scent created a wonderfully calming atmosphere. She felt an overwhelming desire to enter the pool. She slipped out of her jeans and tee shirt, folding them neatly before shoving them into her backpack, the fabric crumpling slightly as it settled among the other contents. With a practiced motion, she draped her bomber jacket over the top of the pack. Inside the backpack, her weapons were carefully stowed away. She eased herself into the water, the lukewarm water enveloping her like a gentle embrace,

allowing her to savor the serene atmosphere that surrounded the pool. Lost in her thoughts, she relished the peacefulness, unaware that beneath the shimmering surface, a hidden threat lay in wait. The contrast between her blissful ignorance and the lurking danger created an unsettling tension, as the water, which felt so inviting, concealed secrets that could change everything in an instant. Aleena looked around and smiled.

"Maybe I should stay here. It seems safe," she thought. She has no idea that something is approaching her from deep beneath the water, emerging from a hidden tunnel she doesn't even know exists. She is at the edge of the pool, cherished memories of home and family danced through her mind, filling her with a sense of nostalgia and comfort. A soft smile shadowed her face. Just as she was lost in those happy thoughts, a sudden disturbance rippled across the water's surface from the other end of the pool. With a jolt, she turned to see a horrific creature emerging from the depths, its form breaking through the calmness of the pool. The contrast between her serene recollections and the looming threat before her was stark, leaving her heart racing as she tried to comprehend the surreal scene unfolding right in front of her. As she hoisted herself up and over the edge, the creature, initially oblivious to her presence, suddenly shifted its focus.

Its piercing gaze locked onto her, and in that instant, a primal instinct seemed to awaken within it. The air around them thickened with tension as it unleashed a bone-chilling screech that echoed through the surroundings, reverberating off the walls and sending a shiver down her spine. Aleena could feel her heart racing, the adrenaline coursing through her veins as she realized the danger she was in. As she pivoted to snatch her backpack, ready to bolt at a moment's notice, Eli suddenly emerged from behind her, extending a hand in a protective gesture.

"Stay behind me," he instructed firmly, his voice steady despite the chaos around them. With a determined look in his eyes, he drew his pistol, the weight of it familiar in his grip, and took aim. The sharp crack of gunfire echoed in the air as he squeezed the trigger multiple times, each shot a desperate attempt to fend off the creature. The creature let out a piercing scream that echoed through the air before it plunged back into the depths of the water, disappearing into the dark tunnel beneath. Aleena, overwhelmed by the sudden shock and fear, felt her knees buckle as the adrenaline surged through her body, nearly causing her to lose consciousness. Eli is quick to react, he wrapped his arms around her, providing a steady embrace that helped ground her in the chaos of the moment. The water rippled ominously where the creature had

vanished, leaving a lingering sense of dread in the air as they both tried to process what had just happened. He looked at her with concern, asking softly, “Are you okay?” She gave him a slight nod, but as she became aware of her surroundings, a wave of embarrassment washed over her; she is still dressed only in her bra and panties. Her cheeks turned a deep shade of crimson, and before she could fully process the situation, Eli swiftly reached for her bomber jacket, draping it around her shoulders with a protective gesture. Her mind was racing, struggling to piece together the events that had led her to this moment.

“I don’t know what happened,” she murmured, her voice barely above a whisper, trailing off as confusion clouded her thoughts. “I was in a daze of some sort,” she elaborated. He smiled warmly, relief washing over him as he pulled her into another embrace.

"I'm really glad to have found you," he murmured, his voice filled with sincerity. After a moment, he gently suggested, "We should probably get moving now." She nodded in agreement, her expression shifting to one of determination. She retrieved her jeans and her weathered tee shirt from her bag and slipped into them. As she fastened the weapon holster snugly around her waist, they exchanged a determined glance, a silent agreement passing between them. With a shared sense of purpose, they stepped forward into the unknown.

21

The Final Steps

Aleena and Eli have traversed through the labyrinthine levels of the ominous realm known as the Backrooms. They encounter an array of surreal environments, each more bizarre than the last. As they delve deeper into the Backrooms, the bond between them strengthens. As they ventured deeper into the Backrooms, they found themselves in a strange room. Surrounded by an endless array of mirrors that lined the walls. The reflections were mesmerizing yet disorienting; each time they moved, their mirrored counterparts seemed to lag or twist in unexpected ways, creating a surreal dance that defied the laws of reality. It was as if the room had a mind of its own, playing tricks on their senses and making it nearly impossible to find a clear path forward. With every step, they had to concentrate not only on their own movements but also on deciphering the erratic behavior of their reflections, which seemed to mock them with their uncanny, delayed responses. The atmosphere was thick with unsettling energy, amplifying their confusion and heightening their awareness of the bizarre nature of this particular level. Aleena caught sight of her reflection in one of the mirrors, and to her astonishment, it was grinning back at her, even though her own lips remained firmly

pressed together. The smile on her reflection was unnaturally wide, stretching from one side of her face to the other. A chill ran down her spine as she processed the bizarre sight, and she turned to Eli, her voice a mix of fear and disbelief. “Did you see that?” she exclaimed, her heart racing as she pointed back at the mirror, hoping he had witnessed the strange phenomenon alongside her. He glanced nervously at the reflections surrounding them, his brow furrowing with concern.

“Don’t look at them," he urged, his voice tinged with anxiety. "We need to find a way out of here." The atmosphere felt heavy, and the flickering lights only added to the unease. He could sense the weight of the situation pressing down on them. With a determined look, he turned away from the glassy surfaces, ready to search for an exit, hoping to find a way out before the unsettling reflections could draw them into the mirrors. Aleena glanced away from her reflection, a mix of uncertainty and hope flickering in her eyes as she posed the question, “Do you think we’ll find a door?” Her voice was tinged with a hint of anxiety, as if the very thought of facing what lay ahead was daunting. Eli, sensing her trepidation, offered a reassuring smile, his confidence unwavering.

“Yes, I believe we will,” he replied, his tone steady and encouraging. “But we need to keep moving forward; the door is out there, waiting for us to

discover it." His words hung in the air, a promise of possibility that urged them to press on. As they trek through the labyrinthine mirror room, Eli grasped Aleena's hand firmly, their senses heightened with each cautious step. The reflections danced around them, creating an almost dizzying effect, but Eli's attention was drawn to a large rectangular mirror that loomed ahead, its dimensions reminiscent of a door. He exchanged a glance with her, and in that silent moment, they both understood the unspoken possibility: this mirror might just be their escape route.

The air was thick with anticipation as they approached. The primary obstacle is the door itself, and it seems to beckon them closer with the allure of their own images. Eli and Aleena are acutely aware of the danger lurking behind that shimmering facade. They understand that if they were to approach too closely, the enchanting reflections would reach out and draw them into the mysterious realm of the mirror world. This realization hangs heavily in the air, a silent agreement between them as they stand at a safe distance, their hearts racing with both curiosity and caution. Their alternate reflections reach through the mirror in an attempt to pull one of them in.

Aleena swung her blade with precision, the edge biting into the arm of her reflection, only to recoil in shock as a similar wound manifested on her own skin. The sudden realization sent a jolt of adrenaline through her, and she gasped in disbelief, her heart pounding in her chest. Her gaze flicked to Eli, who stood motionless, his expression a mix of concern and astonishment as he processed the implications of their

predicament. "This complicates things," he murmured, his voice steady despite the tension in the air. He leaned closer to inspect her arm; worry etched across his face. Aleena took a deep breath, attempting to dismiss his concern.

“I’m fine,” she insisted, though the sting of the cut was undeniable. Eli nodded, his eyes still lingering on her injury.

"It isn’t deep, but you certainly have a deadly aim," he commented, a hint of admiration creeping into his tone. She rolled her eyes, a smirk playing on her lips as she surveyed the yellow-tinted room with mirrors. “It may seem like we’re in a vast space filled with mirrors, but…” she paused, uncertainty creeping into her voice, “are we really?” Eli's brow furrowed in confusion; his gaze locked onto hers as he tried to decipher the enigma of their surroundings. Eli turned to Aleena, curiosity evident in his voice as he asked, “What are you thinking?”

“Let’s keep moving, I have my suspicions,” she responded. Aleena subtly directed her gaze toward the far side of the room, hinting at something intriguing. They both began to walk toward a wall adorned with mirrors, their reflections flickering in the glass as they moved closer. However, just as they neared the surface, an unexpected shift caught their attention, causing them to pause and exchange puzzled glances. As the wall in front of them began to recede, it transformed into a long, narrow hallway that was eerily absent of mirrors. Eli and Aleena exchanged a quick glance, a mix of determination and fear flashing in their eyes. They sprinted past the reflections trapped within the mirrors.

Their reflections erupted into a cacophony of desperate screams, their faces contorted in anguish, as they reached out, trying to break free from their glass prisons. The sound echoed in the air, a haunting reminder of the danger they were leaving behind, urging them to move faster as they plunged into the unknown. But as they ran through the hallway, the walls began to take on a yellowish shade.

22

The Other Side

As Eli and Aleena strolled deeper into the seemingly endless corridor, their eyes were drawn to a bright yellow door gleaming at the far end. Aleena's finger shot out, directing Eli's attention to the door, her excitement palpable. Eli, however, responded with a heavy sigh, a mix of weariness and determination evident in his voice.

"Let's head over there," he suggested, his tone hinting at both curiosity and a hint of reluctance as they prepared to navigate the long stretch of hallway that lay before them. They stepped forward together, their movements careful and deliberate as they approached the door. When they finally stood before it, Eli felt a lump in his throat and hesitated for a moment before slowly turning the knob. As they crossed the threshold, the world around them shifted abruptly, and they found themselves once again ensnared in the familiar, disorienting yellow maze. Aleena's voice broke the silence, filled with despair as she exclaimed, "No!"

Eli felt a wave of dread wash over him, his heart heavy with the weight of their predicament. In an attempt, to comfort her, he reassured her, "We'll find a way out, I promise," though he could sense the tension thickening in the air. Aleena, lost in her thoughts, replied with a hint of resignation, "We're

never going to leave this place," her words echoing the fear that loomed over them both. Eli turned and embraced her. She started crying. He gulped. "Look, we'll find a way," he said as he looked into her eyes. She softly nodded. As they pressed onward, time slipped away, and the once vibrant yellow maze lay eerily still around them. Unlike their previous encounter with the maze, there were no lurking creatures ready to pounce. Leaving an unsettling silence that hung heavily in the air. Aleena suspects that they are in a different part of the Backrooms. The emptiness felt foreboding, as if the very walls were holding their breath, waiting for something sinister to awaken. Aleena leaned closer, her voice barely above a whisper as she said, "This isn't like the first time." Eli met her gaze, a silent understanding passing between them. He inhaled deeply, feeling the weight of the moment settle in his chest, and instinctively tightened his grip on her hand. The thought of her suddenly opening a door and vanishing into another part of the Backrooms sent a shiver down his spine; if that happened, he knew he wouldn't hesitate to follow her, no matter where it led. The air around them felt charged with unspoken fears and hopes, and in that shared silence, they both understood the stakes of what lay ahead. They stumbled upon a weathered wooden crate. Curiosity piqued, he knelt and pried it open, revealing the items inside--two bottles of refreshing almond water and a neatly packed box of energy bars. The sight of the unexpected find sparked a moment of silent exchange between Eli and Aleena, their eyes locking in a shared understanding of the situation.

With a slight grin, Eli broke the silence, suggesting, "I guess we better take these," recognizing the potential for a much-needed boost on their journey ahead. They stashed the bottles and some energy bars into their backpacks, knowing they might come in handy later. “We might need these," Aleena said, glancing at Eli as they resumed their journey. They trekked for what seemed like forever, Aleena could feel the fatigue settling into her legs, each step becoming a little more laborious than the last. Eli, on the other hand, was doing his best to mask his own exhaustion, but Aleena could easily see through his facade. The way he shifted his weight and the slight grimace that crossed his face betrayed him, revealing that both were feeling the strain of their journey.

23

A Deeper Connection

She proposed that they find a quiet spot to rest and grab a bite to eat. As they wandered in search of a secluded room, they noticed a red arrow spray-painted on the wall, directing them down the hallway to the left. They continued and soon found a white door. Eli opened it cautiously, and they stepped inside. This door led to a different hallway, one that wasn't the yellow maze. As they walked further, they noticed office rooms lining both sides, but it was clear that no one was around. They were completely alone. They moved quietly, trying not to make a sound as they explored. Eventually, they discovered an unlocked door and stepped inside. Eli quickly pulled the blinds shut.

"I think we should stay here for a bit," he suggested. His proposal elicited a heavy sigh from Aleena; her expression clouded with unease. After a moment of contemplation, she acquiesced with a nod, and they settled down to enjoy the almond water and the energy bars they found. As they munched on their snacks, Aleena turned to Eli, her curiosity piqued. "Eli, what made you come searching for me?" she asked, her voice tinged with a mix of concern and intrigue. He grinned and responded, "The town was

disappearing, and when I learned that you had left, I felt compelled to follow you. It was a long shot, really, to think I might actually find you, but something deep inside me believed it was meant to be. I like to think that fate played a hand in bringing us together."

As he finished, Aleena felt a rush of warmth spread across her cheeks, a blush igniting at the unexpected depth of his words. "Eli, once we manage to escape the chaos of the Backrooms, you need to return to your own life, and I must do the same," she said, her voice trailing off as she contemplated the weight of their circumstances. After a brief pause, she continued, expressing her gratitude, "I truly value your company; it feels almost a miracle that we found each other in such a bizarre place, but…"

Eli quickly interjected, sensing the underlying tension in her words, "But you're concerned that I might disrupt your quiet life." Aleena offered a friendly smile, suggesting they could always stay connected through Facebook. He chuckled lightly, a mix of amusement and acceptance in his expression.

"Of course," he replied, but beneath the surface, Aleena felt a knot of anxiety tightening in her stomach. The thought of Eli returning with her filled her with dread; she knew that if he did, the media would seize the opportunity to spin wild tales, thrusting her into an unwanted spotlight. The pressure of public scrutiny loomed large, and she found herself grappling with how her absence would invite a flurry of speculation. The last thing she wanted was to be the center of attention, especially when the truth of her situation was far more complicated than anyone

could imagine. They really can't share where they've been; no one would believe their story about the Backrooms. She's uncertain about what awaits her upon returning, but she's certain it's going to be chaotic. Eli is probably feeling the same way. The office was furnished with a simple desk and a faux suede black futon that could be transformed into a small bed. They placed their backpacks beside the futon. Eli had taken the precaution of locking the door, anxious about the possibility of an unexpected interruption while they indulged in some much-needed rest. The atmosphere was quiet, almost serene, as they settled in, hoping to recharge before facing whatever challenges lay ahead. Aleena found herself questioning the wisdom of trying to catch some sleep, especially given the circumstances. With the almond water they had consumed earlier and the energy bars that were supposed to provide a quick boost, she wasn't convinced that either of them would be able to drift off at all. The combination of these two seemed to promise more energy than relaxation, leaving her feeling a bit restless. She glanced at her companion, wondering if they were both feeling the same buzz of alertness, and whether it was even worth attempting to close their eyes for a moment of rest. The uncertainty of sleep loomed over her like a cloud, making her second-guess the decision to even try. They both shut their eyes, yet fatigue was no

longer a concern for them. *"Damn it,"* Aleena pondered. Eli wrapped his arms around her, creating a sense of comfort as they lay together in silence. Although sleep eluded them, they remained in that stillness, lost in their thoughts. Questions swirled in their minds about their lives, the choices that had led them to the Backrooms, and the uncertainty of whether they would ever find their way back home. The weight of their conundrum created a bittersweet blend of hope and despair.

24

Saying Goodbye to the Backrooms

Aleena and Eli navigated the yellow maze, where the flickering fluorescent lights and the old peeling floral wallpaper felt less intimidating than their first encounter in the Backrooms. Surprisingly, they hadn't encountered any entities or creatures, but rather than feeling reassured, their senses were heightened. They couldn't shake the feeling that the moment they let their guard down, something would emerge from the shadows. They traversed the corridors of the office level, their footsteps echoing ominously as they found themselves in the yellow maze once again. Occasionally, they pause, seeking refuge from the oppressive atmosphere that seemed to close in around them. In a hidden nook of the non-Euclidean maze, they gathered closely, finding solace in one another's presence amidst the unsettling surroundings. The air was thick with an unspoken bond, a shared understanding of their situation that enveloped them, as they exchanged hushed words and fleeting glances, each moment a fragile respite from the chaos that lay beyond their secluded haven. Eli leaned closer to Aleena, his voice barely above a whisper as he shared his playful suggestion. Aleena's eyes widened in surprise, her expression a mix of disbelief and curiosity as she turned to face him fully. "What?" she exclaimed, her shock evident in the way

her brow furrowed, and her mouth fell slightly open. With a mischievous glint in his eye, Eli continued, "I was thinking we could revisit some of the fun we had before we left the colony," punctuating his words with a cheeky wink that hinted at shared memories and the intimacy they once shared. “Eli, I’m not sure,” she hesitated, her voice trailing off as uncertainty filled the air. “We need to remain vigilant.” He nodded in agreement; the seriousness of the moment reflected in his eyes. Then, without warning, he leaned in and pressed his lips against hers in a passionate kiss that seemed to erase all doubt. It was wrong and dangerous to let their guard down, but Aleena missed being held and comforted, she needed support, and Eli would give it to her. The world around them faded away as they melted into each other’s embrace, their bodies instinctively drawing closer. The kiss deepened, igniting a spark that quickly transformed into a fervent exploration of desire, as they lost themselves in the warmth of each other’s touch, savoring the intimacy that enveloped them. As they lay entwined in each other's arms, the world outside seemed to fade away, leaving only the warmth of their shared intimacy. The peaceful atmosphere wrapped around them like a soft blanket, but suddenly, a noise shattered the tranquility, pulling them back to reality. Aleena's voice broke the silence, barely above a whisper as she asked, "What was that?" Eli felt a lump form in his throat, a mix of

surprise and concern washed over him. With a sense of urgency, he suggested, "Let's get dressed," knowing that the comfort of their moment was now overshadowed by an unsettling thought of something approaching. Once they had dressed, they cautiously stepped out and walked onward. The air felt thick with tension, and they exchanged anxious glances, each silently fearing that an Eldritch horror might emerge from the shadows at any moment, ready to pounce. Each step felt like a gamble, as they braced themselves for whatever might lurk just beyond their sight. They wandered through a seemingly endless maze of hallways and rooms, surprisingly not encountering any dark entities along the way. Eli glanced around, uncertainty flickering in his eyes as he remarked, "I'm not sure what that noise was earlier, but we should probably keep looking for another door." He hesitated for a moment, his thoughts trailing off as they rounded a corner. Just ahead, a vibrant yellow door caught their attention, illuminated by a buzzing neon sign above the door that boldly proclaimed, "Exit." The sight of it sparked a flicker of hope in Eli's chest, as he wondered if they might finally be lucky enough to find a way out of the Backrooms. They hesitated at the door, worrying that turning the knob would lead to disappointment on the other side. Both have endured their own unique trials while navigating the treacherous expanse of the Backrooms, a place where reality bends and sanity teeters on the edge. The looming door before them holds the promise of escape, yet it also carries the weight of uncertainty; if it fails to lead them to their desired destination, the consequences could shatter

their minds and souls beyond repair. "Are you ready?" he asked, his voice steady despite the tension in the air. Aleena met his gaze and nodded; a silent agreement forged in shared fear and determination. Just as they prepared to step forward, a chilling, inhuman howl echoed through the dimly lit corridors, sending a shiver down their spines and reminding them of the lurking dangers that awaited them. They were acutely aware that the creature lurking in the shadows could very well be a Hound, yet the prospect of escaping the torment of their current existence was too enticing to ignore. Each passing moment felt like a countdown, a relentless reminder that time was slipping away, and with it, their chances of breaking free from the suffocating confines of the Backrooms diminished. The air was thick with tension, the thought of remaining trapped in this nightmarish labyrinth was unbearable, driving them to seize the fleeting opportunity before it vanished entirely. Eli swung the door open with a sense of urgency, and they stepped into an alley. As they turned back, the door was gone. Aleena glanced at Eli, her eyes reflecting a mix of curiosity and apprehension as he gently clasped her hand in his, giving her a reassuring nod. Together, they made their way toward the mouth of the alley, where the sounds of the city began to envelop them. Stepping out from the shadows, they find themselves in a vibrant new world that feels both exhilarating and surreal. The street ahead was alive with cars, bustling pedestrians, and the distant chatter of conversations, creating a lively backdrop that pulsed with energy. Their hearts raced with excitement as they realized they were home, though it

took a moment for the reality to sink in. Aleena exclaimed in delight, “Oh my god, we’re home,” and they shared a warm embrace before strolling down the sidewalk, soaking in the atmosphere and the lively energy of those around them. Aleena’s wide smile was contagious; Eli began smiling too. The sunlight bathes everything in a warm glow, illuminating the familiar sights of *San Diego* that stretch out before them. People bustling about, engaged in their daily routines, while the sound of laughter and conversation fills the air. The scent of the ocean wafts in from nearby, mingling with the aroma of street food from vendors lining the sidewalks.

As they take in the scene, the contrast between the darkness of the Backrooms they left behind and the lively atmosphere around them is striking, making this moment feel like a fresh start, a chance to embrace the ordinary yet beautiful rhythm of life. Eli turned to Aleena, curiosity etched on his face as he asked, “What will you do now?”

She hesitated, beginning to respond, “I must go home and…” but her words faded into silence as her gaze fell upon a vibrant poster plastered on a wall. It featured a band named *Mystic,* and a wave of recognition washed over her, reminding her that the group was originally called *Mystique*. The lead singer, with her striking dark brown hair cascading over her shoulders and piercing blue eyes, was dressed in an eye-catching gothic ensemble that seemed to exude an air of mystery; Aleena couldn’t help but mutter to herself, “I don’t remember her looking that way before,” as she pondered the transformation of both the band and the memories

that accompanied it. Eli raised an eyebrow, curiosity etched across his face as he asked, “What is it?” In response, she simply shook her head, a gentle smile gracing her lips as she turned to face him. Despite the uncertainty bubbling beneath the surface, she chose to dismiss the warning signs that were becoming increasingly apparent.

As she locked eyes with her surroundings, a hint of doubt flickered in her eyes, signaling that something was off. Perhaps it was the prolonged time spent in the Backrooms that had her on high alert, making her instinctively wary of the unexpected and everything she sees, but something seemed off. Despite her efforts to stay calm, an unsettling feeling lingered, urging her to remain cautious.

Eli squeezed her hand and said, “Don’t worry, we’re home.” He wrapped his arm around her, and she exhaled. “Aleena, I need to make a call and hopefully I can catch up on current events since we’ve been gone.” Two women who are in their 30’s passed by, and Eli smiled at them in a flirtatious manner, but they ignored him, looking at him as if he was one of the homeless. He just assumed that his scruffy appearance was the cause for their caution. Aleena looked at him with a raised eyebrow and she scoffed. “I guess some things don’t change,” she remarked. Eli let out a light laugh. As they strolled down the sidewalk, Eli and Aleena stumbled upon a booth that resembled a photo booth. Curiosity piqued, Eli stepped inside and quickly realized it was a free charging booth for cell phones. He raised an eyebrow and pulled Aleena in with him. "What is it?" she asked, her eyes widening at the electronic panel. She

scanned the instructions displayed above, exclaiming, "This is a charging booth for smartphones. Wow, cool!" Unbeknownst to them, a small print below the instructions held a date that would have left them devastated. Aleena still had her phone, but after everything that had happened, she was skeptical about its functionality; it would be a miracle if it worked. Eli encouraged her to give it a try, but she hesitated, explaining that her phone had been dead for quite some time, resting lifelessly in her backpack.

"It's free to charge, just try it," he insisted. With a mix of hope and skepticism, she retrieved her phone, noting the cracks on its surface. As she placed it on the charging pad, a flicker of life returned to the screen. Aleena glanced outside the booth, observing the stream of people passing by, oblivious to her presence. Her attention shifted to the cars around them, all of which appeared to be electric. It struck her as strange; she distinctly remembered a time when gas vehicles were common too. A chill ran down her spine, an unsettling feeling that something was off, lingering in her mind. "Your phone's charged," Eli announced, breaking her train of thought. She took it off the pad and scrolled through her contacts. She called her parents, but her sister answered.

25

Other World

As soon as Aleena recognized her sister's voice on the line, she hurriedly introduced herself.

"Oh my god, Aleena," her sister gasped, a mix of surprise and concern evident in her tone. "Where are you?" Aleena quickly explained that she was at one of the phone charging booths, and her sister assured her that she would come to pick her up. Unsure of her surroundings, Aleena mentioned the name of the business located near the booth to help her sister find them. After a brief wait of about twenty minutes, an electric blue sedan pulled up alongside the curb. Aleena and Eli emerged from the booth, and she slid into the front passenger seat while Eli settled in the back. Her sister's curiosity piqued as she glanced at Eli, asking, "Who's he?" Aleena swallowed hard, introducing Eli as her friend while casting a quick glance back at him. Her sister's surprise was evident as she exclaimed, "Wow, I thought you were still with Tyler." Confused, Aleena asked, "Tyler who?" This only deepened her sister's bewilderment.

"We definitely need to talk when we get home," her sister replied. Not wanting to interrupt their family moment, Eli requested to be dropped off at an old mistress's apartment complex. When they reached the apartment complex, Aleena hesitated, asking, "Are

you sure you want to be dropped off here?" He reassured her, "It's fine. Just give me your number, and I'll call you later." He leaned in to give her a gentle kiss that made her cheeks flush. She quickly jotted down her number along with her parents' contact information. She urged him to reach out if he needed anything, and he simply nodded in response. When Aleena and her sister got home, she quickly realized their parents weren't there.

"Where are they?" she asked, prompting her sister to give her a puzzled look.

"Mom's in Puerto Vallarta, remember?" her sister replied.

"Just humor me," Aleena insisted. As her sister opened the fridge for a Bud Light, Aleena dropped her backpack on the couch and scanned the room. Her eyes landing on a family photo featuring a man she didn't recognize. Turning to Kim, she noticed her light brown hair was longer than she remembered, it was tied back in a ponytail, and she was wearing denim overalls. A rainbow-colored friendship bracelet adorned Kim's wrist, but Aleena didn't think much of it. "Kim, who's next to Mom?" she asked, causing Kimberly's jaw to drop in shock.

"Oh my god, Aleena, you did forget everything, didn't you?" she exclaimed, but Aleena just chuckled, realizing her sister was serious.

"He's the reason you left over ten years ago," Kimberly explained, and Aleena's expression shifted to one of horror. "What happened between us?" she asked, her curiosity piqued. Aleena pressed on, her voice tinged with concern. "This isn't funny; you're really freaking me out," Kim, rolling her eyes,

decided to indulge her sister. “Alright, let’s play along. Three years after Dad passed away from a heart attack, Mom reconnected with a man from high school. You didn’t approve; it felt too soon for her to start dating again, which led to a big fight between you two. That’s when you left with Tyler, your boyfriend. I still remember your last message: *Kimmie, I’m sorry, but I’m moving to Europe with Tyler.* Occasionally, I’d hear from you, but then the texts just stopped five years after you left. I knew you were still out there, alive somewhere, so I wasn’t too worried. Mom ended up moving to Puerto Vallarta with Javier after he retired, and she let me stay here as long as I needed. I’ve been here ever since, always hoping you’d come back.” Kim’s eyes looked down, letting out a heavy sigh, before meeting Aleena’s earnestly. The information that her sister gave her was overwhelming. Her dad is dead, and her mom is with a stranger living at a retirement community down south. She sighed, “I remember now,” Aleena said, though she did not entirely remember anything. It was as though she stepped into an alternate reality. In fact, she is certain she did.

“Now it’s your turn,” Kim said. Aleena sighed, acknowledging the complexity of her situation.

"I need a shower and some food first," she told Kim, who nodded and quickly ordered delivery. As Aleena made her way to her room, she noticed it looked pretty much the same, except for a new poster of her favorite band, now spelled, *Mystic,* hanging on the wall. She paused to admire it before grabbing a few clothes that still fit and headed to the bathroom. After her shower, she took a moment to check herself out in

the mirror, relieved to see no strange doppelganger lurking within it, she stepped back into the living room and found Kim about to call their mom.

"Hold on, just hold on before you call her," Aleena urged. Kim nodded in agreement. The doorbell rang, and the Ring camera revealed a delivery person, dressed in a red polo shirt and jeans.

"Pizza's here," Kim announced. After placing the pizza on the table, they settled down to eat.

"I got you a mushroom and spinach pizza, just how you like it." Aleena looked at her curiously. She doesn't have strong pizza preferences and is curious as to why her sister mentioned it, but she brushed it off.

"So, what's the story? Who was that guy? And how come you look just like you did ten years ago? You must have some secret to staying young. Look at me—I definitely look older." Aleena studied her sister closely. Her sister is three years her junior. If Aleena was 21 when she vanished, she is now 31. Glancing at the calendar by the fridge, Aleena noted it was March 3rd, 2035. A wave of sadness crossed her face as she sighed, realizing that she is in fact in an alternate reality. A wave of bewilderment grazed her face. Then she composed herself.

"Kim, I need you to listen to me because what I'm about to share might sound crazy." Aleena recounted her experiences in the Backrooms, but Kim raised an eyebrow and laughed lightly. "So, you're keeping secrets, but at least you've identified that older man—Eli Marsh. He's not the richest man in the world, though." Kim stood up and grabbed a magazine from the magazine rack on the wall and handed it to

Aleena. “Avery Marsh?” Aleena whispered in surprise. “Yeah, he’s the wealthiest man in the world. I can see why you’d think Eli is connected; he resembles him, kinda,” Kim explained. Aleena felt a knot in her stomach. *“Oh no, Eli doesn’t know,”* Aleena muttered, sighing heavily.

“If you’re not ready to share everything, that’s okay. I’m just glad you’re back and hopefully you are here to stay. I missed you,” Kim said, pulling Aleena into a warm embrace. Wiping away her tears, Aleena felt the weight of the moment. Later, as she lay in bed staring at the ceiling, her thoughts drifted to Eli and how he was faring.

26

No Turning Back

After a particularly disheartening encounter with his estranged mistress, Eli found himself at a homeless housing complex, a place that felt like a far cry from the life he once knew. He tried to contact his wife, but the number did not exist. The memory of his friend/former mistress's words to the police still echoed in his mind: *"It's one of those Unknowns."* Those words linger, a reminder of how easily one can slip into the shadows of society, becoming just another face in the crowd, lost and overlooked. He assumed that she was just being a bitch but something in her eyes indicated that she truly did not recognize him. Eli stood there, feeling utterly lost and bewildered, as a nagging sense of something being off washed over him. It struck him that everything had changed the moment he and Aleena crossed over to this new reality. After being settled into a homeless housing complex, he began to piece together the fragments of his disorientation and was hit with a staggering revelation: it was now the year 2035. The weight of this discovery left him reeling, as he grappled with the implications of the time slip. The world around him felt both familiar and alien, filled with advancements and changes that he could hardly comprehend. Each day brought new surprises, and Eli couldn't shake the feeling that he was not just in a

different place, but in a completely different reality, where the rules he once knew no longer applied. He glanced at the calendar once again, the year 2035 staring back at him, and muttered to himself, “Ten years have passed, while I was in the Backrooms, unbelievable.” It was a strange realization for him. Later, as he stood in line at the cafeteria of the homeless shelter, the smell of warm food wafting through the air, he turned to the server with a grin and declared, “Hey, I’m Eli Marsh, I’m the richest man in the world.” The words rolled off his tongue with a hint of irony, a playful jab at the stark contrast between his current situation and the grandiosity of his claim. In that moment, the server shook her head. The plus size woman with short blonde hair and grey eyes, wearing an off-white apron, raised an eyebrow and let out a soft chuckle.

“Oh, really?” she said, pausing for a moment before handing him a steaming bowl of chicken soup that she had just ladled from a large aluminum pot. With a resigned sigh, he settled down at one of the cafeteria tables, ready to dig in. As he enjoyed his meal, curiosity got the better of him, and he inquired about who the richest man in the world is. To his astonishment, someone mentioned the name Avery Marsh. *“Avery Marsh? That’s my younger brother,”* he thought to himself, a mix of surprise and pride washing over him. He swallowed hard, his mind racing, and then asked if anyone had a picture of him,

eager to see what his brother had become. Eli was taken aback when a man showed him the latest issue of People magazine, featuring his brother on the cover as the most influential entrepreneur of 2035. As he read the article, he was stunned to discover that it referred to Avery as the only child of Rena and Timothy Marsh. The revelation hit him hard, and he felt as if he might faint. With a ghostly expression, he quietly murmured, "I was never born."

"Keep dreaming, loser, there's no way you're rich. Just stop pretending to be someone you're not. If you were really rich, you wouldn't be hanging around here, you delusional fool." The man who had handed him the magazine, chuckled dismissively before striding away, leaving Eli feeling a mix of embarrassment and frustration. As the laughter faded, Eli's mind drifted to the thoughts of Aleena, her smile and warmth contrasting sharply with the harsh words he had just heard. He couldn't shake the feeling that her belief in him was the only thing keeping him afloat in a world that was not his world.

****

When Aleena awoke the next morning, she walked into the bathroom to take a shower. She looked in the mirror and noticed her face had changed, she looks older, by ten years. Her mouth dropped but her sudden age change wasn't what shocked her. She looked down at her stomach; a prominent pregnant belly replaced her flat one. She screamed. Kimberly knocked on the door. "What's wrong?" Aleena opened the door and to Kim's surprise she saw Aleena's changed body.

Aleena put her robe on and walked into the Livingroom, in shock. Oh my god, I'm pregnant, no," she said, clearly in distress. She sat on the couch and her sister sat next to her. They were both in shock. "No, this is too weird," Kim said. "Suddenly you are pregnant. How the Hell?" "Now, do you believe me," Aleena told her. Kim slowly nodded, "There are no words," she said, as she stared at her sister's pregnant belly. "I don't know what comes next, but we'll figure this out together. You're not alone," Kim reassured her sister, determined to support her through this unexpected journey. Aleena gave a slight nod. Kim, contemplating the weight of her sister's situation asked, "Should I let mom know that you're back and expecting?" her voice tinged with concern. With a heavy sigh, Aleena replied, "Just give me some time to process everything, alright?" The weeks ahead have been hard on Aleena. She has kept the details of her mysterious disappearance and unexpected pregnancy to herself, even from the doctor. Her sister is the only one that knows the truth. She feels that revealing the full story isn't necessary; after all, aside from her sister, she doubts anyone else will truly understand or believe the truth of what happened during those lost years. Meanwhile, Eli is currently living in a homeless apartment complex, but he's found work assisting a gardener. Unlike Aleena, he lacks an ID and is being paid in cash under the table.

To establish his new life, he's considering paying someone to create an ID for him, even though it feels a bit sketchy. However, he feels it's a necessary step to make this fresh start truly his own. There were a couple of times when he wanted to call Aleena but decided against because he wanted to give her time to reunite with her family.

Months later, Aleena welcomed a healthy baby girl into the world. Her mother only knew that Aleena had spent ten years abroad with her boyfriend and had returned with a child. Despite her initial disappointment over Aleena's long absence, she was thrilled to embrace her new role as a grandmother. A year passed, and Aleena found herself working as a waitress at a local restaurant when a man walked in who resembled Eli, albeit older. She couldn't help but stare, and when he noticed her gaze, their expressions mirrored surprise. He approached her and enveloped her in a warm, tight hug.

"Aleena, oh my god, how have you been? I'm so sorry I didn't call you. Trust me I really wanted to but," he paused. Aleena cut in, "But you found out that you no longer are the man you use to be, right?" She guided him to one of the empty booths, and they sat down. She gulped and sighed. He nodded, and their eyes met, silently acknowledging the secret they held. Eli had transitioned from being just a gardener to running his own gardening business, which provided a decent income, though it was far from the comfortable life he once knew. As he opened up about his struggles, she reciprocated with her own. Just then, her sister stepped in with Aleena's one-year- old daughter in a stroller.

"Hey, there you are. Linette wants to see her mommy," Kim said, casting a disapproving glance at Eli. "So, you found him, I see." Her tone was icy, laced with resentment, as she knows Eli is the father and couldn't fathom why he hadn't reached out to Aleena all this time. Eli swallowed hard, feeling the weight of her words.

"Thanks for bringing her," Aleena picked up her daughter out of the stroller and hugged her, giving her a kiss on the cheek. She turned the baby so she could face Eli.

"Eli Marsh, this is your daughter, Linette." Eli's jaw dropped in disbelief. He was at a loss for words. "Yeah, she's your daughter, so you better make good and be a father," Kim took a better look at him. "Wow, really sis, he's much older than you, mom's gonna flip."

"I'll deal with that when the time comes," Aleena responded. *A week later,* Eli decided to move into Aleena's parent's home, with her mother still living in Puerto Vallarta, Aleena felt it was the right thing to do. Kim wasn't too happy about it, but she accepted Aleena's decision. The house has six bedrooms and before Eli moved in, it was just her and her sister. Later, during dinner, Kim confided in her sister about her new girlfriend, mentioning that there was a possibility she might move in with them. Eli glanced at Aleena, who appeared taken aback by the revelation. Aleena vividly recalled her sister not being a lesbian in the other reality, she identified as straight. Struggling to reconcile this new information, Aleena managed to express her support, albeit with a hint of confusion lingering in her voice.

"Well, I'm happy for you," she said, trying to mask her bewilderment over Kim's unexpected shift in orientation. Curiosity piqued, Kim then asked, "Was the other me a lesbian?" Aleena responded with a shake of her head, emphasizing the stark contrast between the two realities. Aleena smiled as she said she was happy to be home with her family, reaching out to take her sister and Eli's hand. Her daughter, perched in a highchair, giggled joyfully. Later that evening, as Kim and Aleena's daughter drifted off to sleep, Aleena and Eli shared a warm embrace in her full-size bed, they chatted quietly.

"Was your sister gay in the other reality?" Aleena shook her head, reflecting on how the world might look the same yet hold subtle differences. Aleena's voice trembled as she spoke, revealing the weight of her emotions.

"This reality is hard for me to accept," she confessed softly. Eli nodded in agreement, his expression mirroring her turmoil.

"I can't believe that my brother, Avery, has taken my place, and I was never born," he added, a hint of disbelief lacing his words. Aleena let out a subtle scoff, a bittersweet smile breaking through her somber mood. "I understand. The friends I attended Comicon with before I vanished have since moved on; one has relocated to Washington, while the other is happily married and settled down in Texas." She turned to Eli, her eyes searching for his reassurance. He gently caressed her cheek, grounding her in the moment. "Eli, do you think we can truly adapt to this new life? Can we ever move past the pain of our past?" she asked, vulnerability evident in her voice.

Eli responded with determination, "We will, and we must embrace what we have now."

Six years have passed, and Aleena's daughter is now thriving in school, while Kim and her wife have settled into a comfortable life with Aleena and Eli. Eli continues to run his small business, relishing the peace that comes with stepping away from the intense scrutiny of being a billionaire and in the spotlight. Life seems idyllic, filled with the joys of family and the satisfaction of personal success. However, beneath the surface of this happiness, both Aleena and Eli occasionally find themselves haunted by the shadows of their past, where their dreams can morph into unsettling nightmares that draw them back to the eerie memories of their time in the Backrooms. As Aleena wandered through the local art gallery one afternoon, she stumbled upon an intriguing painting that immediately captured her attention. Two women were perched on a bench in front of it, engrossed in conversation as they gazed at the artwork. They discussed the art-piece. The painting itself, a stunning beach scene, meticulously crafted on a four-piece rectangular canvas measuring eighteen by forty-four inches, popped out. The vibrant colors and serene waves seemed to invite viewers into a tranquil paradise. Aleena felt relaxed and it gave her a sense of peace. However, as Aleena stood there, enjoying the painting, she noticed something unsettling. The idyllic beach landscape began to shift and distort right before her eyes, morphing into the unsettling yellow

maze of the Backrooms. The transformation was both mesmerizing and disconcerting. Her heart raced as she instinctively took a step back, her mouth agape in shock. In an instant, the image before her shifted back to a serene beach landscape just as quickly. "Did you see that?" Aleena asked one of the women, her voice tinged with urgency. They turned to her, their expressions perplexed by her question.

"See what?" asked the woman with dark blonde hair, clearly puzzled. Aleena felt a wave of embarrassment wash over her for even bringing it up, yet she needed validation for what she had just experienced.

"It looks like a landscape of the beach," replied the other woman, who had curly hair, her tone dismissive. Aleena swallowed hard, nodding in response, and quietly walked away. When she found Eli, she recounted her strange encounter, he enveloped her in a comforting hug.

"I didn't want to tell you, but I've seen it too," he confessed, his voice low. "I've caught glimpses of that terrifying place—once in a mirror and another time when I opened a door at work. It was there for just a second before it vanished." In that moment, they both understood that the haunting memories of the Backrooms would linger with them for the rest of their lives, an inescapable shadow that would forever be with them, in a distant memory or perhaps just waiting for them beyond the veil.

Step lightly, tread with care,
For if you slip from reality's snare,
You might find yourself in the Backroom's embrace,
Where damp carpets linger, a foul trace.
Mono-yellow madness fills the air,
Fluorescent lights hum, a constant glare,
Endless rooms stretch, a maze of despair,
Six hundred million miles, a haunting lair.
If you sense a presence lurking near,
Pray for Mercy, for it's drawn to your fear,
Pray for Mercy and flee if you can escape with all your might, in this twisted realm, there's no end in sight.

Author's Notes

The inspiration for this novel originated from a short story I shared on Wattpad and AO3. Titled, "The Maze from Hell," it follows the journey of two individuals from vastly different backgrounds as they find themselves trapped in the unsettling, non-Euclidean nightmare known as the **Backrooms.**

In a pocket dimension, beyond our familiar world, there exists a shadowy and merciless environment teeming with dark mysterious creatures and countless dangers. The main characters in this book navigate mercilessly through the unknown. Amidst the eerie expanse of the Backrooms, the couple unexpectedly cross paths, forging a bond as they journey through the perils together. After the characters finally escape the Backrooms, they find themselves in an alternate reality. As the author, I decided to place them in this new setting because it would be virtually impossible for anyone to return to the exact universe they left behind when they entered the Backrooms. I might be off base, but as a writer, it's fascinating to ponder the possibility of a place like the Backrooms actually existing. The mere idea of a place like the Backrooms could disrupt our understanding of reality itself, sending ripples through the very essence of existence, is chilling. In the first chapter, titled *"The Peasant Girl,"* we are introduced to Aleena, a character who embodies the everyday struggles of a common citizen, contrasting sharply with Eli, who comes from a wealthy background. As the story unfolds, Eli ultimately achieves his desire for a life away from the public eye, finding a solution to his troubles.

Interestingly, it is Aleena who guides him toward this alternate reality, possessing the extraordinary ability to traverse different realms, a gift she remains unaware of throughout her life. This dynamic between the two characters highlights the intersection of privilege and the hidden potential within those who seem ordinary. As the years pass, they share their lives and grow old together while raising their daughter, yet the lingering dread of waking up to find themselves trapped in the Backrooms again will forever shadow their existence—until they die.

<u>What happened to the people in the colony?</u>
After Eli and Aleena left, the town continued to disappear, taking its inhabitants with it, except for Syra and Kyle. They realized what was happening and escaped the chaos. As they were once Raiders who navigated various levels of the Backrooms before arriving at the colony, it's likely that they are still alive somewhere in that strange realm, possibly thriving in another colony. The rest of the people had vanished only to reappear in other levels of the Backrooms. Their fate sealed.

<u>Who deserves to be in the Backrooms?</u>
No one, but it seems that the Backrooms have a way of drawing in individuals who have committed various wrongdoings. While some people may accidentally find themselves in this strange, non-Euclidean realm, it often feels like a trap designed to ensnare both the virtuous and the wicked alike.

Unknown Dimensions

When Aleena and Eli made their escape from the Backrooms into an alternate reality, Eli found himself in a world where he had never been born. This absence meant he had to acquire an ID and other essential documents through dubious means to lead a normal life. Despite the questionable origins of his paperwork, he managed to live an ordinary life, passing away years later, in his 90s. Aleena passed away in her 90's as well. Their daughter stumbled upon her mother's journal, which contained the closely guarded secret of the Backrooms. Inspired by the revelations, she transformed the story into a novel titled *Unknown Dimensions*, categorizing it as fiction to ensure its acceptance, knowing that people would not believe the truth if presented as non-fiction. Those who have read the story of Aleena and Eli ultimately provided solace for others grappling with their own experiences after escaping the Backrooms.

About the Author

CG Heandez was raised in Orange County, California, where her passion for storytelling began to take root. In the 1990s, she entered marriage, yet her aspiration to craft narratives remained a constant driving force in her life. Ultimately, she achieved her lifelong ambition of becoming a published author, a dream she has successfully realized. Her literary works are available across various platforms, including Amazon, the Kindle Store, and numerous other online retailers. Since the 1990s, she has committed herself to the art of writing, diligently working towards her goals and making significant strides in her literary career.

Books by CG Heandez

FLARE

A Time Traveler's Companion
Women's Stories: A Collection of Unbelievable Short Stories

The Maze from Hell: A Backrooms Tale

My Immortal: The Doctor & Me
(A Fanfiction)

Other Books by the Author under the *pename,* ***Cecile Garcia***

Chandra's Quest
In the Company of Elves
Saints and Sinners: Affairs of the Heart
The Stranger Things: Paranormal, Supernatural and Unusual Phenomenon
Lost in the Backrooms: The Phoenix Files vol. 1
Life of a Dasher
Secret Diary of a Gypsy Heart
Author's Notes: Personal Notes Based on the Author's Books

www.ingramcontent.com/pod-product-compliance
Lightning Source LLC
LaVergne TN
LVHW010616100826
845148LV00014B/2996

* 9 7 9 8 2 3 4 0 1 3 2 3 1 *